1963

This book may be kept

CLASSIC TALES

FROM

SPANISH AMERICA

SELECTED, EDITED AND TRANSLATED

BY

WILLIAM E. COLFORD

GREAT NECK　　　　　　NEW YORK

TABLE OF CONTENTS

For my daughter, Esperança

¡Oh Rey! Es mi poema la exposición sonora
donde hallaréis mi fauna, donde hallaréis mi flora:
racimos de bananos y plumas de avestruz.

Llaneros, gauchos, indios; aquí, los hombres rojos;
y cuando de mis tierras se cansen vuestros ojos,
podéis mirar mis cielos en donde está la Cruz.

Santos Chocano: A.S.M.C. ALFONSO XIII

INTRODUCTION

As the twentieth century draws to its close, more inhabitants of the Western Hemisphere will be speaking Spanish than English. In appraising the literary production of the New World, therefore, the serious student of Comparative Literature must take into account the tremendous strides made during this century by writers who use the Spanish language to interpret the American scene. Hispanic America has issued its declaration of cultural independence: its literature has come of age, and is speaking in a bold, clear voice for all to hear.

During the colonial period in the Americas there was a far richer literature written in Spanish than in English, particularly in poetry, both epic and lyric. England's great Elizabethan Age had come to maturity even before the first North American colonies were established, yet there was nothing written in Anglo-America to compare with the stirring accounts of Hernán Cortés and Bernal Díaz del Castillo describing the conquest of Moctezuma's empire, the sweeping epic poem *La Araucana* by Alonso de Ercilla about the campaigns in Chile, the nostalgic commentaries of Garcilaso de la Vega concerning the Inca culture in Peru, or the lovely lyrics of Sor Juana Inés de la Cruz in Mexico.

Only with the advent of Emerson, Thoreau, Poe, Hawthorne, Melville and Whitman did North American literature reach its full flowering; and by the second half of the nineteenth century — when relative stability had come to Spanish

America after the long wars for Independence and the ensuing civil conflicts — the new Latin republics had produced a constellation of literary stars of equal magnitude: Domingo Faustino Sarmiento and José Hernández in the Argentine, Alberto Blest Gana in Chile, Juan Montalvo in Ecuador, Ricardo Palma in Peru, José Asunción Silva in Colombia, Rubén Darío in Nicaragua, Manuel Gutiérrez Nájera in Mexico and José Martí in Cuba. Moreover, it should be borne in mind that in the other great Hispanic language — Portuguese — Brazil was producing major literary works that are beyond the scope of this present volume.

But it is in the twentieth century that all forms of literature have forged ahead in Latin America. As education has been extended both in breadth and in depth, there has been a rapid growth of a discriminating and highly literate reading public. Poetry and the novel have flourished as never before, and the short story has come to be one of the principal media of contemporary literary expression. It is to give the North American reader some insight into the scope of this genre in Spanish-speaking America that these representative stories have been translated into English.

Mathematicians tell us that the whole is equal to the sum of its parts. But a nation is greater than the sum of its natural resources, its manpower, and its industrial potential; there is an intangible something, an almost mystic interaction between man and the land that is particularly strong in Latin America. One of the two dominant themes in its literature has always been Man against Nature. But as the twentieth century advances, Man against Man is coming to the fore as the other dominant theme: the struggle against his hostile physical environment is giving way as a source of literary inspiration to man's struggle against his social environment.

If you were asked to pick a score of short stories that would give the Latin American reader an insight into the heritage and culture of the United States, how would you proceed? In all probability you would select stories written by representative authors from different regions: the Old South, the Middle West, the mountainous mining regions, the West Coast, traditional New England, the cattle country of the Southwest, and several large cities like New York, Chicago and San Francisco.

The plan of presentation in this book, therefore, is to depict regions rather than countries, since geographic and ethnic factors are even more basic in the life and letters of Latin America than they are in the literature of the United States. The fact that no story from Ecuador (for example) is included in this collection does not mean that there are not splendid writers in that country; it means simply that the Andean region is already represented by Bolivia and Peru. Similarly, the many countries of Central America are represented by Nicaragua's Rubén Darío, the historic region of Gran Colombia by Venezuela's Uslar Pietri, and so on.

The problem in presenting a collection of *cuentos criollos* — typical Spanish American short stories — is not what to include but what to leave out, so outstanding is this type of literature today. Moreover, there was difficulty in choosing among the many excellent tales written by the authors who were finally included; in the case of the prolific Ricardo Palma of Peru and the trenchant Manuel Rojas of Chile, the only solution was to translate two stories from each which illustrate different facets of their brilliant work.

All the authors are twentieth-century writers, though many — of course — were born in the nineteenth. Some of the stories selected are gay, others tragic; some light and fanciful, others starkly realistic. And woven into the fabric of many of them, through the deep green of the tropical jungle and the bleak brown of the Andean altiplano, runs the blood-red thread of violence.

The subject-matter of the stories covers a wide range: soldiers in colonial Peru and in nineteenth-century Mexico, present-day miners and railroad workers in the snow-covered Andes, missionaries in the steaming jungles of Venezuela, stevedores in coastal Chile, sugar workers and revolutionaries in Cuba, horsemen of the Argentine pampa, Indians in lofty Bolivia, city dwellers in several contemporary capitals. All the tales are favorites of anthologists, and many have appeared in collections of short stories edited for Spanish American literature in the original language. They are here translated, and collected for the first time in a volume expressly prepared for students of Comparative Literature.

This introduction will not be extended here to include a detailed discussion of each of the authors and his place in the development of the Spanish American short story; such comment is better reserved for the pages immediately preceding each selection, where the background of the region, the writer and his period will be presented. We shall begin at the southern tip of the continent — in Chile. Then, after some typical stories of the rugged Andes and the rolling pampas, we shall make our way northward through Peru and the northern part of the continent to Central America and the highlands of Mexico. From there we shall go down into the Caribbean, concluding with the Commonwealth of Puerto Rico, which forms the natural bridge between the two American cultures.

W.E.C

New York, 1962.

Manuel Rojas

1896-

was born in Buenos Aires of Chilean parents. Handsome, well-built and vigorous, he worked hard at several manual occupations during his youth, which was spent in Argentina and in Chile: as a laborer on the mighty trans-Andean railroad, as a sailor, and as a stevedore on the docks in Valparaiso. The characters in his stories are often drawn from these youthful experiences.

In 1924 he settled definitely in Santiago de Chile and devoted himself to journalism and creative writing. His first collection of short stories, Hombres del sur (Men of the South), was published there in 1926 and won him immediate recognition as one of the most gifted and forceful writers of the rising generation. It is from this collection that our first story is taken.

That same year he published his first novelette, and five years later his novel Lanchas en la bahía (Boats in the Bay) was awarded first prize by La Nación of Santiago. In 1931 he became Director of the

University of Chile Press. Señor Rojas has since widened his reputation as one of Latin America's most outstanding authors. He is past president of the Society of Chilean Writers.

Though most of his central figures are rugged men like himself, he can capture equally well the inner feelings of more sensitive persons such as the unnamed young man in our second story, The Glass of Milk. Perhaps it is autobiographical in some of its details. This profoundly simple tale, all the more effective for the great restraint with which it is told, is typical of Manuel Rojas' quiet authority as Chile's master craftsman in the art of the short story.

THE CUB

* * *

I

THE ENGINE GAVE a short blast on its whistle, and big, red-checkered handkerchiefs waved in the train windows. There were shouts of farewell, and the train started off, creaking as it went.

Standing on a small mound of hard-packed snow, Jeria, the foreman of the track gang, and Antonio (nicknamed "Fuzzy" because of his hair, which was twisted and tangled like a blackberry thicket) watched the train pull away and go down the grade. It was a tiny, new train that looked like a toy as it rolled along gaily on the narrow-gauge track; the funicular cog between the rails resembled a long spine with iron vertebrae.

It was the second train out of Las Cuevas, the last station on the trans-Andean line, bound for Los Andes, the first town on the Chilean side of the border. At the windows swarthy faces smiled as they passed by the two railroad employes.

"Good-bye, Don Máximo!"

"Good-bye, boys!"

Jeria called them "boys" but every one of the men was taller than he. Taller, because anyone crossing the continent from ocean to ocean and seeing that track that climbs from the vineyards of Mendoza and goes through fields, over mountains, across bridges, around curves, over ravines and through that endless tunnel, cannot believe it has all been built by men five feet five inches tall, with small

3

chests. No. That must have been done by tall men with broad, deep-sounding chests like tree trunks, with strong legs ending in feet that never slipped on the hard rocks, and with thick, muscular arms that picked and hammered their way into the tunnel bore, where the dynamite exploded with muffled detonations.

Those "boys" were these men. Now that the mighty work on the trans-Andean railroad was finished, they were emigrating to Chile in groups that would scatter among the nitrate fields in the north, the seaports on the Pacific coast, and the copper mines in the center of that country.

When the last car disappeared around the curve, Máximo and Antonio came down from their little vantage point. All the bystanders, employes of the railroad and the police, had returned to their houses and canvas shelters. Máximo lighted a cigarette, turned up the collar of his thick overcoat, stamped his feet, and spoke:

"We're the only ones who are staying."

"The only ones. . . ."

The only ones, because they had come there with the men who were leaving. Máximo was staying now because he was in love with a brunette from Mendoza, a charming girl, simple-hearted and sincere. Antonio was staying, too; the eyes of María, daughter of the foreman of Puente del Inca, had tamed his adventurous spirit.

The two men had been travelling around together for a long time. At one period it made no difference to them whether they went in one direction or another: all roads were good, and at journey's end there were pretty girls, ports open to all the sea lanes of the world, broad cities and deep seas. Now, two women were holding back those men who had been to all the Pacific ports of South America, from Balboa, full of Negroes, to the Straits of Magellan, full of Alacalufe Indians. . . .

2

AN ICY WIND was beginning to blow. The sky was overcast, and it looked like snow. Suddenly, as he approached a mound of snow, Máximo stopped. He narrowed his eyes and looked upward; his somewhat near-sighted gaze fell upon a form huddled on top of a pile of railroad ties.

"What's that?"

"The kid. . . ."

"*El Lloica's* boy?"

"Vicente!"

At the sound of his name he raised his head and showed his face — the young face of a child, but already weather-beaten in appearance and serious in its expression.

"What are you doing here?"

"Nothing. . . ."

"Didn't you go to Chile?"

"What for? I don't know anybody . . . I have no family. It's all the same to me whether I go or stay."

He spoke with the conviction and assurance of a grown man. He was eleven years old, slender and big-boned, and gave promise of becoming a tall, muscular man, quiet and resolute.

"What are you going to do now?"

"I don't know."

Máximo and Antonio looked at each other. Vicente was the son of one of the many miners who had worked on the tunnel construction job. He was called *"El Lloica,"* the Indian name for a small Chilean bird with a red breast. Manuel Martínez received this nickname because he wore a red Bolivian poncho that came down to his waist and made him look like a gigantic *lloica*.

A gambler and a fighter, a tireless worker, *El Lloica* was

liked by the brave, the timid, and the ordinary workers, because no one ever saw him bully a weak man, shrink before a bold one, or hold back when the work was hard and
strong men were needed. When pay day came, *El Lloica*
would settle his debts, put some money aside as savings,
take his son by the hand, and seek out some nearby blanket
on which the cards showed their tempting figures and the
dark hands of the track workers scooped in their gambling
bets.

Manuel gambled because he liked it; he played just for
the joy of it. If he won, he would pick up his money, take
his son by the hand, and go off to bed — for the card games
used to last as long as two days. If he lost, he would shrug
his shoulders, take a drink of brandy, and go off to bed just
the same. And his son, quiet and thin, with mended trousers so outgrown that they came halfway up his legs, would
stay close to his father and take care of him, going to get
him something to eat or drink. Stretched out on his own
black poncho and rolled up in his father's red one, he
would fall off to sleep at his father's feet.

His mother was dead; he had never known her. Always,
as long as he could remember, he had gone around only
with his father, that big, brawny man, strong and swarthy,
who walked like a bear and had inexhaustible strength. His
father was agile, too, and had sight so keen it permitted
him to parry knife thrusts at the very edge of his sombrero
when duelling for fun, armed with a short stick, while the
boy, armed with a penknife, would quit with sore ribs, tired
of finding *El Lloica's* guard always ready against his quick
thrusts. He was a full-blooded racial type — a pure South
American, from his straight, dark hair to his thin ankles and
broad-soled feet.

One pay day, in a tent camp pitched beside the railroad
right of way, *El Lloica* placed his final bet and had his last

drink of brandy. The game had been going on since six o'clock in the evening. At about midnight a fight broke out. A track worker from Rioja, a puma hunter by trade (according to him) and a bandit by choice (according to everybody else), tried to run off with someone else's money. *El Lloica* seized him by the hand, squeezing it so hard the fingers crunched, and made him drop the handful of bills he had taken. The man from Rioja didn't like to waste words, and said ironically as he walked out, "We'll see each other later. . . ."

The game continued, but half an hour later a pistol shot brought them all to their feet. A voice shouted: "Outside!"

El Lloica started to go, but they stopped him: "Don't go out, Manuel."

"What do you mean, 'Don't go out,' when they are challenging us?"

Vicente, pale but dry-eyed, stood there motionless beside his father. When Manuel went out, the brightness of the snow in the night disclosed the bandit standing about three yards away, facing the door, waiting for him. A long knife gleamed in his hand, and three toughs formed a bodyguard behind him.

The man from Rioja said, "I'm waiting to find out if you're as brave out here as in there. . . ."

Everyone went out behind Manuel, and some placed themselves beside him, ready to fight; but *El Lloica,* spreading his arms, made them step back:

"No, friends. This card game is for me alone. I'm the dealer, and I have the bank. Here's the first card!"

He reached for his belt and drew out a broad steel blade which he held at arm's length.

"Dad!"

It was Vicente. He wasn't pleading, but he seemed to be reminding his father that he had a claim on his life, and that his father ought to think of him before fighting. But *El Lloica* was sure of himself, and turning toward his son, said to him:

"Don't worry, my boy."

In fact, there was no need to worry. He sprang forward to within one yard of the man, who raised his hand with the dagger in it and began to make a complicated series of feints which ended by stabbing at the grinning face of Manuel Martínez. *El Lloica* leaned to one side, and the blow went whistling by. . . .

Only the tip of his own knife was visible, protruding beneath his black hat. He never struck to inflict a wound in the face; for him, knife fights were battles to the death, and he struck at the center of the body, aiming for the stomach or the heart. Consequently, within two minutes the bandit's coat was slit up the left side, caught by a knife thrust from bottom to top. He answered with a slash capable of cutting off a puma's head, and the top of *El Lloica's* hat went flying through the air. But Manuel Martínez was a calm man, and did not lose his patience.

No one spoke. The others looked on without daring to shout, for fear a word might distract the fighters. Suddenly the man from Rioja bent over, lashed out quickly, and delivered a thrust that grazed *El Lloica's* trousers and drew a few drops of blood from his right leg, which he had put forward. *El Lloica* bristled with indignation. It is all very well for a man to defend himself and use any tricks to inflict a wound, but he doesn't strike at the legs; let him strike at the face or the body: he is fighting with a man, not with an animal. In less than a second the fight was over. *El Lloica* advanced boldly, swung his arm in a wide circle, closed in to the center of it, and from there lunged straight forward like a steel spring to plunge his knife deep into the stomach of the bandit, who fell with his arms spread wide apart.

At that moment someone shouted: "The police!"

Everyone disappeared. The wounded man lay stretched upon the ground, and from there he was carried away. The investigation began: nobody knew anything. But at four in the morning, those who were awake that night heard shots far away. They had come upon *El Lloica* just as he was fleeing into Chile, and since no one dared come close to him they chose to shoot him down from a distance. Vicente's screams told the police that his father had been hit. When they reached his side *El Lloica* was dying, struck by three bullets.

The sergeant was hit by a stone that almost knocked him over. "Coward!" shouted Vicente as he sprang furiously at his face, scratching him. They had to tie the boy up to keep him still.

El Lloica died the following day. Vicente, an orphan now, wandered through the camp, dry-eyed, refusing food. The workers called to him, spoke to him in gruff and open-hearted terms about his father — "a fine, brave man" — and tried to cheer him up. He lived with them until the work was ended. And like those injured birds that cannot go with the flock that is flying off, Vicente stayed on alone when the men left for the cities. Indifferent to his fate, he was resigned to anything in the solitude of the mountains. He was the flowering, the offspring of that muster of mighty men who were leaving on the tiny new train that looked like a toy. . . .

3

VICENTE WAS TAKEN in by Máximo and Antonio, and when they moved away he was adopted by the work gang. As he was the only boy in the camp, he was called affectionately "the kid," a name which stuck to him. On this account, several years later when Vicente had turned eighteen he was still called by the same nickname despite his height, which exceeded that of the tallest man by four inches.

He was the mascot of the gang. He was liked because of the memory of his father, and because he was quiet and obedient. Vicente worked at everything: he would wash the workers' clothes, sew their patches that were coming loose, and brew their *mate** the way they liked it with brandy in the winter, while outside the snow piled up as high as forty feet.

When he was nineteen a foreman at Las Leñas, a small station near Puente del Inca, gave him a job as a track inspector. His work was simple: it consisted of examining the condition of the right of way from Las Leñas to Las Cuevas. Every morning at ten o'clock there would appear around a curve in the line the tall figure of "the kid." Wearing boots, a pair of corduroy pants to protect his legs, a jacket of the same material with leather trimmings, and carrying an iron-tipped staff, he would go through the camp amid the greetings of the workers:

"Hello, kid. . . ."

"Hello, old timer. . . ."

El Aguilucho, an old worker, would stop him, look at him, and embrace him: "What a fine big fellow you've become! You look like your father, you tiger cub!"

The old man would grow nostalgic, and "the kid," slapping him on the back, would continue his trip. An hour later he would pass by again on his way back.

"What a strapping fellow! He topped his father by eight inches!"

"That type is disappearing. Real men, as fine as pure gold or copper!"

* *Yerba Mate,* a strong tea (sometimes called Paraguayan tea) drunk in the southern countries of South America.

Everyone marvelled at the way he ordered his life: his conduct was exemplary. He never gambled, hardly ever drank, and was level-headed. Nevertheless, deep down in his eyes the remembrance of his father lived on, and sometimes when he was angry the spirit of the dead *Lloica* came through so clearly that the workers saw his father again in his resolute actions.

At eighteen he had fallen in love with the daughter of the foreman, who knew him well and did not hesitate in giving him the girl's hand in marriage. As Vicente had saved up some money and dearly loved Ana, it was decided to set the wedding for an early date.

But like the tiger cub he was, he was bound to be of the same breed: the father's fate stalked the son. Vicente, off duty one Sunday, left happily — almost gaily — for Las Cuevas. He joined a friend, and they went to the inn to drink a glass of wine. Sergeant Chaparro was there, a burly fellow as strong as Vicente, swarthy and sullen. Vicente did not greet him because he had never forgotten that the sergeant was the one who had ordered the volley that killed his father; and though he harbored no feeling for vengeance, he felt no friendship toward him. But Sergeant Chaparro had moments when he was in a bad humor, and that day he stopped Vicente in the middle of the room:

"Why don't you say hello to me?"

"I have never said hello to you, sergeant; you shouldn't be surprised at that."

"You hate me because I arrested your father. . . ."

"My father wasn't arrested, he was murdered!"

"He had wounded a man. . . ."

"Face to face, all by himself . . . not like you; four of you ganged up to shoot him in the back. . . ."

"Don't be insolent!"

"You spoke to me, and I'm answering you. . . ."

For men like those workers, everything was a question of virile strength and courage: the law, when it won, was good; if not, it was useless. Therefore, the sergeant raised his saber and struck Vicente on the shoulder with the hilt.

"Sergeant!"

"What's wrong with you?"

"Remember, I am my father's son. . . ."

"All the worse for you!"

And again the saber struck the shoulder of "the kid," who lunged at him with such force that the sergeant fell back on top of a table and slid down to the floor with a crash. Everybody stood up. Someone said:

"Pretty good, for a little shove. . . ."

But the sergeant called the guard, and "the kid" was taken away with his arms tied behind him, powerless to defend himself.

What happened afterward no one ever found out, but two days later Ana, Vicente's sweetheart, as well as everyone else on the platform of the little station, saw him at the window of a second-class coach on the express train as it went through. He smiled, but the smile on his pale, drawn face showed pain.

When he returned from the hospital he had lost his timid and respectful manner; and though he gave no sign of looking for trouble, everyone realized that the blood of Manuel Martínez, *El Lloica,* flowed again through the veins of the tiger's cub.

But he was no longer a cub: his claws had grown in misfortune, and rage had sharpened his instinct for revenge. When he walked past Chaparro, he looked like a young jaguar that glances sideways but is getting ready to spring straight forward.

Vicente married. He gave up his old job and took another which was just the same but with a different stretch of track, from Las Cuevas to the middle of the trunnel. Patiently he awaited the day of his revenge. He knew it was something preordained by Fate: it had to happen. Had he not done it, he would not have been able to live with himself, and the memory of his father would have shamed him.

4

ONE MORNING a little before noon, as he was about to enter the tunnel on his regular trip, he sighted Sergeant Chaparro, who grinned when he saw him.

"How are things with you, my brave young fellow?"

"Not as well as with you, you murderer!"

The sergeant advanced, but Vicente Martínez had his plan all prepared. He threw his oil lamp at the sergeant's face, and plunged into the tunnel. Fifty yards inside, where it was dark, he stopped and drew from beneath his corduroy jacket the dagger that belonged to his father. It had been made out of a doubled-edged file, smooth and sharp as a razor, and had been set into a hilt made of pieces of copper and iron, inlaid with bone.

The sergeant kept on coming into the tunnel, straining to see in the darkness. Vicente hid in one of the many niches in the tunnel walls, and from there he saw, silhouetted against the light, the figure of the man who was stalking him. He let the sergeant go by, and then spoke:

"I could fight you and kill you face to face, but I prefer to kill you from the back so that my offense will be greater and my vengeance will match your crime . . . !"

For the first time in his life Chaparro knew fear. His revolver pierced the darkness with its flashes of light, but it was useless. A laugh rang out, and *El Lloica's* old dagger plunged through the sergeant's left shoulder, aiming straight for the heart.

The rest was a question of time. Two days later Vicente Martínez was in Valparaiso, and the broad expanse of the sea lay open before his tiger eyes.

THE GLASS OF MILK

* * *

T HE SAILOR, who was leaning against the starboard rail, seemed to be waiting for someone. In his left hand he held a bundle wrapped in a piece of white paper that showed grease spots in several places; with the other hand he puffed on his pipe.

A thin young man came out from behind some freight cars, stopped a moment, looked toward the sea, and then continued walking along the edge of the dock with his hands in his pockets, unconcerned or lost in thought.

When he drew opposite the ship the sailor shouted to him in English:

"I say! Look here!"

The young man raised his head, and without stopping answered in the same language:

"Hello! What?"

"Are you hungry?"

There was a short silence, during which the youth seemed to be thinking; he even took one step shorter than the others, as if he were going to stop. But finally, smiling sadly at the seaman, he said, "No. I am not hungry. Thank you, sailor."

"Very well."

The sailor took his pipe from his mouth, spat, put the pipe between his lips again, and looked away. The youth, ashamed that his appearance should arouse feelings of charity, seemed to quicken his pace, as if he were afraid he might think better of his negative answer.

A moment later an impressive tramp with blue eyes and a big, blond beard, who was dressed outlandishly in ragged clothes and huge, broken shoes, walked in front of the sailor. The latter, without calling him over first, shouted at him:

"Are you hungry?"

The question had not even been completed when the loafer, looking with gleaming eyes at the package the sailor held in his hands, answered quickly:

"Yes, sir; I am very much hungry."

The sailor smiled. The package flew through the air and landed in the eager hands of the hungry man, who did not even thank him. Opening the bundle, which was still slightly warm, he sat down on the ground and rubbed his hands in glee as he saw its contents. A dockside derelict may not know English, but he would never forgive himself for not knowing enough to ask anyone who speaks that language for something to eat.

The young man who had gone by a few minutes before witnessed the scene from where he was standing a short distance away. He was hungry. He had not eaten for exactly three days, three long days. And more from timidity and shame than because of his pride, he shrank from standing in front of steamer gangplanks at mealtime waiting for the sailors' generosity in order to get some package containing left-over food or scraps of meat. He could never do that; he would never be able to do it. And when, as in the recent incident, someone offered him his leftovers, he would decline them heroically, but with regret, because refusing made him even hungrier.

For six days he had been wandering through the alleys and along the docks of that port. He had been left there by an English steamer from Punta Arenas, the port where he had jumped ship, abandoning his job as a cabin boy. He had spent a month in Punta Arenas helping an Austrian crab fisherman in his work. On the first northbound ship he had stowed away.

They found him the first day out, and sent him below to work as a stoker in the boiler room. At the first large port the steamer touched they set him ashore, and there he stayed like a package without a name and address, not knowing anyone, without a penny in his pocket, and without knowing how to work at any trade.

While the steamer was still in port he could eat, but afterwards. . . . The huge city rising beyond the alleyways lined with bars and cheap lodging houses did not attract him; it seemed like slave quarters, without light or air, and without the open grandeur of the sea: behind those high, straight walls people lived and died, stunned by the sordid struggle.

He was possessed by the terrible obsession of the sea, which twists the calmest, most orderly lives as a mighty arm bends a slender rod. Although quite young, he had already made several voyages along the coasts of South America in different ships, working at various jobs and tasks, all of which had practically no application on land.

After the ship left he kept on walking around, trusting to luck to find something just to keep him going until he could get back to his familiar way of life; but he found nothing. There was little activity at the port, and the few ships where there was work didn't sign him on.

The place was full of professional vagabonds wandering around, unemployed sailors like himself, who had jumped ship or were fugitives from the law; loafers resigned to idleness, who kept alive somehow or other by begging or stealing, counting the days like the beads of some grimy rosary, waiting for something extraordinary to happen, or not waiting for anything — men of the strangest and most exotic races and nationalities, even types in whose existence one does not believe until he has seen a living example.

THE NEXT DAY, convinced that he could not last much longer, he decided to try any means to get food. While walking along he came upon a ship that had come in the night before and was loading wheat. A line of men kept walking back and forth across a gangplank carrying heavy sacks on their shoulders from the freight cars up to the hatches of the ship's hold, where the stevedores took over. He stood there watching for a while until he got up courage to speak to the foreman and ask for a job. He was taken on, and quickly joined the long line of loaders.

During the early part of the day he worked well, but later he began to feel weak. As he walked along with the load on his shoulders he felt dizzy, and would sway on the gangplank when he looked down between the side of the ship and the wall of the dock into the frightening chasm where the water, flecked with oil and covered with debris, gurgled softly.

At lunchtime there was a short rest; and while some of the men went to eat in the cheap taverns nearby and others ate what they had brought, he stretched out on the ground, pretending not to be hungry.

He finished the day's work completely exhausted, covered with sweat, and down to his last ounce of strength. While the longshoremen were drifting away he sat down on some large sacks, waiting for the foreman. When the last worker had left, he went up to him; embarrassed and hesitant — though he did not tell him what the trouble was — he asked if they could pay him right away, or if he could possibly have an advance on what he had earned.

The foreman answered that it was customary to pay when the job was over, and that it was still necessary to work the follow day in order to finish loading the ship. Another whole day! Moreover, they weren't advancing a cent!

"But," the foreman told him, "if you need it I could lend you about forty cents . . . that's all I have."

The young man thanked him for the offer with a sorrowful smile, and went away. Suddenly he was seized by a sharp sense of desperation. He was hungry, hungry, hungry! He was so hungry that it doubled him up, just as a blow with a thick, heavy whip might have done. He saw everything through a blue haze, and staggered like a drunken man when he walked. Nevertheless, he would not have been able to moan or cry out, for his suffering was neither acute nor oppressive; it wasn't a pain, but a dull ache, an exhausted feeling; it seemed to him that he was being crushed by a great weight.

Suddenly he felt a kind of burning sensation in the pit of his stomach, and he stopped walking. He kept bending down, down, slowly doubling up like an iron bar being bent by force; he thought he was going to fall. At that moment, as if a window had been opened before him, he saw his home and the countryside around it, his mother's face, and the faces of his brothers and sisters: everything he loved and cherished appeared and disappeared before his eyes, shut with sheer fatigue. . . .

Then, little by little, the giddiness went away; and as his burning stomach gradually cooled, he slowly straightened up. Finally he stood erect, breathing heavily. One more hour and he would fall senseless to the ground.

He quickened his step, as if he were fleeing from a new attack of dizziness, and while walking along he determined to go in and eat anywhere, without paying, ready to be shamed, beaten, jailed, anything. The important thing was to eat, eat, eat. A hundred times his mind kept repeating that word — eat, eat, eat — until the term lost all meaning and left him with a feeling of burning emptiness in his head. He had no intention of running away: he would say to the proprietor, "Señor, I was hungry, hungry, hungry . . . and I have no money to pay. Do what you wish."

HE REACHED the first city blocks, and in one of them found a dairy. It was a bright, clean little shop, full of small, marble-topped tables. Behind the counter stood a blonde lady with a spotless white apron.

He chose that store. The street had little traffic. He could have eaten in one of the cheap taverns near the dock, but they were always full of people drinking and gambling.

In the dairy there was only one patron. He was a little old man with glasses, with his nose buried in the pages of a newspaper. He seemed motionless, reading there, as if he were glued to the chair. On his table was a half-empty glass of milk.

The young man walked up and down on the sidewalk, waiting for him to get out. Little by little he was beginning to feel that burning sensation in his stomach again. He waited five, ten, as much as fifteen minutes. Tired, he stood to one side of the door; from there he looked harshly at the old man.

What the devil could he be reading so intently! He

finally came to imagine that the man was an acquaintance who knew his intentions, and had set out to frustrate them. He felt like going in and saying something rude to make him leave — an insult, or a sentence that would make him understand that a person had no right to sit there reading for such a small purchase.

Finally the patron finished his reading — or at least interrupted it. In one swallow he drank down the rest of the milk in the glass, got up slowly, paid his bill, walked over to the door, and went out. He was a little man, bent with age, who looked like a carpenter or a painter. As soon as he was in the street he adjusted his glasses, stuck his nose in the newspaper again, and walked off slowly, stopping every ten steps to read more carefully.

The young man waited until he was out of sight, and then went in. For a moment he stood at the door, trying to decide where to sit down; finally he picked out a table and went toward it. Halfway there he decided against it, stepped back, bumped into a chair, and then sat down at a corner table.

The lady came over, wiped the table top with a cloth, and with a gentle voice in which there was a trace of a Castilian accent, asked him, "What will you have?"

Without looking at her he answered, "A glass of milk."

"Large?"

"Yes, large."

"Just milk?"

"Is there any sponge cake?"

"No, just vanilla wafers."

"All right, vanilla wafers."

When the lady turned away he rubbed his hands on his knees in cheerful anticipation, like someone who feels cold and is about to have a hot drink.

The lady returned and placed before him a big glass of milk and a plateful of vanilla cookies; then she went back to her place behind the counter.

His first impulse was to drink down the milk in one gulp and then eat the cookies, but immediately he thought better of it; he sensed that the woman's eyes were fixed upon him, watching him curiously. He did not dare to look at her: it seemed to him that if he did so she would become aware of his frame of mind and his shameful intentions, and he would have to get up and leave without tasting what he had ordered.

Slowly he picked up a vanilla wafer, dipped it in the milk, and took a bite; he drank a sip of milk and felt the burning sensation, which had returned to his stomach, diminish and disappear. But at once the reality of his desperate situation rose before him, and something hot and clutching rose from his heart to his throat. He realized that he was going to sob, to sob loudly; and although he knew the lady was looking at him he could not choke back or undo that fiery knot which was growing tighter and tighter. He fought it off, and as he did so he went on eating rapidly, fearfully, afraid that weeping might keep him from eating.

When he finished the milk and cookies his eyes clouded over; something warm rolled down his nose and fell into the glass. A terrible sobbing shook him from head to foot. He rested his head on his hands, and for a long time he wept: he wept with sorrow, with rage, with a longing to weep as though he had never wept before.

HE WAS BENT OVER, weeping, when he felt that a hand was stroking his tired head and a woman's voice with a soft Castilian accent was saying: "Cry, my son; cry. . . ."

A new wave of weeping flooded his eyes with tears, and he cried as forcefully as he had at first, but now not with bitterness but with joy, as he felt a great coolness flood through him, putting out that hot something that had clutched his throat. While he wept it seemed to him that his life and his feelings were being cleansed like a glass beneath a stream of water, and were regaining the brightness and firm texture of other days. When the spell of weeping passed and he was calm again, he wiped his eyes and face with his handkerchief. He raised his head and looked at the lady, but she was no longer looking at him: she was looking out into the street at some far-away point, and her face was sad. . . .

In front of him on the table was a fresh glass of milk and another plate heaped high with wafers. He ate slowly, without thinking about anything, as if nothing had happened, as if he were in his own house and his mother were that lady behind the counter. When he finished, it had already grown dark and the store was lighted by an electric bulb. He sat there a while, thinking about what he would say to the woman when he went out, but nothing appropriate occurred to him.

Finally he rose and said simply, "Thank you very much, señora: good-bye."

"Good-bye, my son," she said.

He went out. The wind from the sea cooled his face, still warm from weeping. He walked aimlessly for a while, and then went down a street that led to the docks. It was a lovely evening, and huge stars were beginning to shine in the summer sky.

He thought of the blonde lady who had treated him so generously, forming plans to repay her and make it up to her in some worthy way when he had money; but these thoughts of gratitude vanished with the warmth of his face until not one was left, and the recent events faded away and became lost in the recesses of his past life.

Suddenly he was surprised to find himself singing something in a soft voice. He straightened up joyfully, and strode along with vigor and determination. He reached the shore and walked up and down buoyantly, feeling himself reborn, as if his scattered inner forces had been reassembled and consolidated. Then the fatigue from his work began to rise in his legs with a slow tingling sensation, and he sat down on a pile of sacks.

He looked at the sea. The lights from the dock and from the ships shone over the water in a red-gold band, shimmering softly. He stretched out on his back, looking up at the sky for a long while. He did not feel like thinking, or singing, or speaking; he felt alive, and that was all.

And he dropped off to sleep, with his face turned toward the sea. . . .

Eduardo Barrios

1884-

*was born in Valparaiso of a Chilean father and a
Peruvian mother. He received his early education in
Lima, and after his family returned to Chile early in
the twentieth century he studied at the Military
School in Santiago. Later he wandered through almost every country in South America, and worked
at widely differing occupations: prospecting, selling
machinery, even weight-lifting in a travelling circus.*

*Señor Barrios finally settled down in Santiago and
devoted himself to literary work. He has since become one of Spanish America's leading novelists and
playwrights, in addition to being a splendid writer
of short stories. In his country's service he has held
such posts as director of the National Library, Secretary of the Chamber of Deputies, and Minister of
Education. In 1946 he was honored with Chile's
equivalent of our Pultizer Prize, the National Award
for Literature. Several of his works have been translated into French, German, English and Portuguese.*

Barrios is a master of the psychological novel, and

portrays with especial skill and subtlety the workings of the overemotional and hypersensitive mind. Madness stalks many of his heroes. His masterpiece in this genre is a keenly penetrating novel about the torments of a monk in a peaceful monastery nestled in Chile's lovely central valley.

In the short story we have translated here, Señor Barrios gives us in his disarmingly simple style an illuminating study of feminine wiles in Santiago society of a few decades ago.

LIKE SISTERS

* * *

IT WAS NINE O'CLOCK in the evening. The cooling scent of a fragrant lotion refreshed the warm air of the room, illuminated more brightly than usual because of Laura's preparations for the theater. The lamp's four bulbs poured forth a flood of light. Against the walls, done all in white, the rococo contours of the Louis XV furniture stood out boldly, along with the countless little pictures and knick-knacks that form part of the gay and delightful decorations in a young lady's room.

A filmy frock splashed a slate-blue streak across the rose-colored counterpane. Margarita, seated in an armchair beside the bed, was waiting for her friend to finish arranging her hair; she was amusing herself by examining an eighteenth-century Venetian fan with the careful attention that time allows for such matters if one has a long wait ahead.

"What a lovely thing! What a charming fan!" she suddenly exclaimed with enthusiasm. "And how perfectly painted!"

"Yes, it is a work of art," replied Laura without turning her head, as she plunged her long, white fingers into her creole-black hair to fluff up her coiffure. Then she added, "I'm not offering to give it to you because it belongs to Mother, but . . ."

"What an idea! Even though it were yours . . ."

They exchanged two or three more sentences just for the sake of conversation, and after that the silence was broken only by the sharp clack of Laura's implements on the marble top of the dressing table as she went along bringing out her natural beauty. With a little lip rouge she accentuated the curve of her mouth, making it ardent and alluring; then she brushed the powder from her lashes, and her eyes glowed in all their smoldering radiance with the dizzying pull of two craters whose dark depths were made compellingly attractive by her fair complexion.

Suddenly there was a knock at the door.

"Who is it?"

"It's me, miss," answered the maid from outside. "A letter for you."

"Margarita, do me a favor and take it; I'm not presentable."

Her friend arose and went over to get the letter.

"It's from Valparaiso," she said as she returned with it.

"Let's see . . . it's Constancia Cabero's handwriting; leave it on the bureau so I can enjoy reading it slowly after I'm dressed."

"Constancia Cabero . . . ," Margarita repeated, as if searching her memory. "Ah! Is she that friend you knew when I met you, the one who used to walk with you and that tall young man in the plaza?"

"That's the one. She's one of my dearest friends — a jewel."

"Very pretty."

"And as warmhearted as she is beautiful."

"She certainly was charming," the other girl said enthusiastically. "There's one thing, though: when I used to see you two together with that young man, I could never quite make out which one of you he was in love with."

"We ourselves didn't know; he courted us both. Imagine!

I don't know . . . if we didn't quarrel over him it was due to the really great, sincere affection we had for each other. When I recall . . ."

"What! So the two of you . . . ?"

"Both of us."

"How amusing! Tell me. Tell me all about it . . ."

Without interrupting her nail polishing, Laura yielded to Margarita's curiosity and began to gather her recollections and piece together the details.

First of all she mentioned Carlos Romero, for that was the suitor's name. A more attractive young man it was impossible to imagine: tall, slender, perfect features, well dressed, distinguished — so much so, that they both felt equally attracted by his big, brown, languid eyes, with long lashes that made his glance so caressing, captivating. . . . Refined and correct in his attentions, he was clearly well versed in the social amenities. As Laura said, he had an inborn refinement of expression, a self confidence, an indefinable delicacy about his gallantry, that brought them extreme and incomparable pleasure, and caused their upbringing, their caution . . . almost their modesty . . . to waver.

They were not unaware of the fact that he was a bit of a gay blade, a night-owl, and that he even had certain rather questionable girl friends; nevertheless, this surrounded him with an aura of boldness which attracted and fascinated them. His type of life, spiced with adventures, indiscreet love affairs and gay parties, held for them — as for the majority of young, unmarried society girls — a mysterious enchantment which was at the same time vexing. In the evening, when they said good-bye to him and thought of the favors that other girls, freer than they, were probably bestowing upon him, they were sad for quite some time, and even sorry they had not permitted him — even just once — some small liberty of the type that strict propriety sternly denies to young ladies. . . .

After these long, thoughtful periods of silence they used to seek each other out, seized by the uncontrollable need to unburden themselves. Then Laura would say, in an outburst of intimacy, "I get such a yearning to be free, to accompany him everywhere . . ."

Constancia would be silent some moments, and would finally add:

"I imagine that those women must be very interesting, very coquettish in their manner, in . . . who knows what! . . . to turn men's heads that way. Believe me, sometimes when I think of them I feel so naive, so lacking in real charm, too severe, strait-laced and sedate in my conduct, and I reach the point where I'd like to break away from . . . No, no! Good Heavens! What I was going to say . . . !"

"No, don't say it. You don't have to tell me; I feel the same way. It's jealousy, sheer jealousy, enough to drive a girl out of her mind."

"With me it isn't jealousy; you know, it's fury — blinding fury. I would exterminate women like that."

"What reason can there be for their existence? They ought to be prohibited."

"That's right!"

These confidences always ended the same way, but they were repeated almost daily. The girls' spirits, alternately rational and raving, rose and fell.

WHEN LAURA, amid adjustments to her corset and rearrangements to her coiffure, had revealed these matters of the heart — somewhat nostalgically — to Margarita, the still-curious friend pressed her:

"Apparently you two girls were both very much in love. And what I really can't understand is why you didn't quarrel."

"Ah!" said Laura warmly. "That would have been impossible between us; we loved each other too much — just like two sisters."

"But sisters quarrel, too, in such cases."

"Well, we didn't. Quite to the contrary. We had agreed that each one of us would do all in her power to make Carlos Romero decide in her favor, but that to influence his decision she would not use any unfair means."

"Ah!"

"So you see, with this agreement there was no room for unpleasantness. Besides — and I repeat this — our friendship was always too strong to have some outsider destroy it."

And Laura continued in this vein, running through the gamut of praise to emphasize their firm friendship. A quarrel between them? Such an absurdity was simply unthinkable. And she concluded by saying, "Even though she had won him, my affection would have been the same as it is today."

"And how did the little flirtation finally end up?" Margarita asked, intrigued, as she held Laura's dress out stiff as a hoop and helped her pull it over her head.

"Pshaw! Nobody won out. Carlos was called to Valparaiso by his father to take charge of his business, and he had to leave Santiago without deciding upon either of us."

"How foolish you two were! The most sensible solution would have been for one of you to step aside."

"What do you expect? It was impossible. We thought of it several times. Once we reached the point of drawing lots, but we immediately cancelled the game, claiming tricks and double dealing; however, I suspect the real reason was that neither of us could stand by indifferently and watch the other make the sacrifice. We loved each other so much. . . ."

Soon Laura finished dressing. Picking up the letter, she went over to the lamp so she could read it better. The fiery brunette's well-developed figure glowed in the stream of light that poured over her low-cut dress, which clung to her hips and fell in gossamer folds.

Holding the letter in her fingers, Laura read in silence; from time to time a smile revealed her sparkling row of teeth. At her side, Margarita gazed at her inquiringly: she was impatiently awaiting the news as her eyes followed the zig-zag of Laura's across the page. The winsome blonde's face was a mirror of her friend's expression: upon it were reflected — by a kind of contagion — the other's grimaces and smiles.

Suddenly Laura's smile ceased to display the glow produced by happiness over pleasant news. First it became hesitant, then bitter, then ironic, indefinable, as her eager pupils enlarged to re-read one passage in the letter. Finally, Laura's arms dropped to her sides: her spirits had plunged to the depths. Her breathing had become labored, and her bosom rose and fell in repressed emotion, as if a storm of wrath were raging within her. A wave of anger swept across her eyes, which flashed darkly. Her lips opened halfway, as if to say something . . . But the girl, taken aback, hesitated a moment. Finally she could no longer contain herself, and her fury exploded in an uncontrollable outburst.

"The deceitful, nasty hussy!" she snapped, clipping each word. "She didn't deserve my affection. The double-dealing, rotten wretch!"

"What's the matter with you? What's going on?" asked Margarita in alarm.

"What disillusionment friends can cause! Just imagine. . . ."

She did not go on. Reason overcame her wrath, and with tears in her eyes she limited herself to the following words, spoken scornfully:

"It's nothing; a betrayal, better forgotten."

She crumpled the letter and threw it in the corner. With a haughty toss of her head to sweep a curl from her forehead, she said as she left:

"I'm going to see if Mother is ready."

Margarita, dumfounded, was unable to account for such a sudden change. Why was Laura, after praising the fine qualities of her friend — her "sister," she had called her — now insulting her?

Invincible female curiosity caused her to forget her good upbringing. Trembling, glancing about her, she picked up the ball of paper, smoothed it out, and read in one of its paragraphs:

"You are probably quite surprised that I have told you nothing about my famous flirtations until now. Well, Laura, all that foolishness is over: I'm engaged. And I'll bet you can't guess who he is? Carlos Romero. The engagement has been formally announced, and the wedding has been set for the first of September. It all happened so suddenly. . . ."

Baldomero Lillo

1867-1923

was the first of Chile's writers to use the short story as a medium of social protest. Much of his background material came from personal observation and participation in mining, which is his country's basic industry. He was raised in the town of Lota, center of the anthracite coal region. (Copper, however, is the principal product of the Chilean section of the Andes.) Like his father, young Baldomero worked for a mining corporation; he had risen to the post of manager of the company store before he left for Santiago to devote himself to writing and to editorial work in the publications section of the University of Chile Press.

Upon his arrival in the capital he was shocked to see the wretched conditions in the slum areas. His stories deal with the social problems of the city workers, with the poverty of the farmers in the Chilean countryside, and especially with the drabness and dangers of the life led by the miners. These themes form the basis for most of the tales in his two collec-

tions, Sub Terra *and* Sub Sole, *published early in the twentieth century. Since that time much progress has been made in Chile, which today is one of Latin America's most forward-looking countries in the matter of social legislation.*

Some of these stories, like the one translated here, use the mines merely as a backdrop for the experiences of the protagonist; others are humorous or satirical; all are full of compassion for the underprivileged.

THE ABYSS

* * *

REJIS, AFTER TAKING from the long row of baskets lined up next to the tunnel wall one that had a tiny, pitted sea shell fastened to the handle, found a place between two thick columns and made ready to satisfy the fierce appetite that five hours of hard work had given him.

It was twelve noon. The workers in that section of the mine kept arriving in small groups, and the lights of their lamps, fastened to the visors of their caps, shone like weird fireflies in the dark, twisting tunnels. Each man, when he reached the row of baskets, took the one that belonged to him and withdrew to his corner to eat his lunch in silence.

For a good quarter of an hour the only sound beneath the black vault was the muffled munching of mouths and the noisy clatter of plates and spoons wielded by rough, invisible hands. Suddenly an isolated voice was heard; many others followed, and lively conversations broke out in the darkness. At the beginning the talk dealt with their work, but little by little the range of conversation kept widening. From one direction came a serious discussion in a low voice; from another, jokes and laughter at the coarse remarks of the wits who were making fun of the oldest man in the gang. He was a poor fellow who always arrived late and had to look for his basket, which the practical jokers would invariably hide so they could call out as he came closer to the hiding place or moved away from it:

"Warm!"

"Cold as an icy stream!"

"Don Lupe is getting scorched! He's on fire!"

All this to the accompaniment of loud guffaws.

Sorry for the old man, who was going back and forth without success, bewildered by all the shouting, Rejis got up and placed the hidden basket into his shaking hands. At the same time he rebuked the cruel jokers forcefully. They answered sharply, and the gloomy cavern was criss-crossed by a brief bombardment of coarse words, which ended in a general burst of laughter following a phrase blurted out by a mocking voice.

In the darkness Rejis' face turned intensely pale beneath the thick mask of coal dust that covered it, and his first impulse was to hurl himself upon the speaker and mete out the punishment justly deserved for the slanderous statement he had made. But a thought flashed through his mind and stopped him as he suddenly recalled a snatch of conversation he had heard that morning as he passed by one of the diggings:

"So Ramón didn't come down again today?"

"It can't be true!"

"I tell you it is. Don Pedro asked about him in the office, and they said he hadn't been in to pick up his identification tags."

Suspicion took root and grew with lightning speed in his brain. Could it possibly be true, what that scoundrel had blurted out so brutally right to his face? Was she deceiving him with Ramón? His face became contorted, and his eyes flashed darkly; shaken, he rose to his feet.

Rejis was a young man of twenty. He was of medium height, and the thinness of his arms and legs, as well as the pallor of his face, attested to the bitter sorrow of a childhood spent down deep in the mines without games, laughter, air, or sunshine. Deeply in love with Delfina, the prettiest and most flirtatious girl in the whole district, he had won out over many rivals who were contending for her hand. One of the most tenacious, and among the last to abandon the field, had been Ramón, a young man his own age. He was a dangerous rival indeed, for he combined with his handsome physical appearance other attractions that made him irresistible to the girls. Rejis, in spite of winning, lived in suspicion and distrust, for his enemy — enraged by defeat — had boasted openly that sooner or later he would get revenge.

Alone in the tunnel, the miner vainly tried to calm down by reassuring himself that it was all nothing but the work of some envious person, and that Ramón's absence might be due to something very different from what the slanderer had implied. But his jealousy, aroused so abruptly, choked off this reasoning, and his only thought was to get out of the mine as soon as possible. Having decided upon this, and without bothering about the basket he had thrown upon the ground, he began to walk quickly toward the exit. While walking he kept working out a plan to get them to allow him to leave the job — quite a difficult matter, for the mine's regulations were strict about this.

The only method would be to make believe he felt ill. But in addition to the repugnance he felt toward lying, there was another obstacle: he would be sent to the surface accompanied by a foreman, whose duty it was to take those claiming illness straight to the infirmary, where they were examined by the doctor or the intern — a wise measure adopted by the administration as a precaution against malingerers. And added to this was the delay involved, which would prevent him from taking the guilty ones by surprise.

Just when he was in despair because of these difficulties and was vainly seeking a way to avoid them, he suddenly stopped, struck by an idea that could save him. With furrowed brow he remained motionless for an instant; then he spun on his heels and turned back, retracing his steps.

He was passing through a broad exit tunnel used for coal cars, and went along stepping over the cross ties that held the steel rails. Suddenly he turned to the right and entered a narrow ventilation duct, steep and very low. Bending over until his hands touched the muddy ground, he climbed up the passageway with great effort and found himself in a tunnel parallel to the one he had just left. It was an old one, out of service, that connected with the mine shaft through an opening placed about thirty yards above the entrance to the main tunnel.

After a few minutes' walk he found himself at the vertical shaft. Standing there on the projecting rim of a rock, he looked down into the black depths from which muffled voices rose with a vague murmur, revealing the presence of miners at the entrance to the corridor. Rejis put out his head lamp so the reflection of its light would not betray him; leaning over a little, and stretching his right hand out into space, he succeeded in touching with the tips of his fingers one of the guy cables upon which the elevator moved up and down.

His plan, although bold and extremely dangerous, was nevertheless very easy to carry out. Within a few minutes lunch hour would be over and the whole mine would resume work. Once the machinery began to move again, the elevator there below him would take its load of mineral to the surface while the other, which was at the top, would come down with the superintendent in it. Since the machinery would then be operating at its slowest speed, he would be able — if he jumped quickly and didn't lose his nerve — to catch the elevator as it passed in front of him and hang on to one of its cross bars. At that hour he was sure of not meeting any of the bosses at the surface, and his absence would pass unnoticed except by a few friends.

Having determined to make the attempt, and with the details of the procedure firmly in mind, he awaited the instant for action with eyes and ears alert. A faint light came up from below and enabled him to make out the gleaming surface of the thin cable attached to the elevator, which was standing motionless at the bottom. Suddenly a very faint noise came up the shaft. Rejis moved slightly, and shivered; his trained ear had detected in those vibrations the tugs on the signal wire informing the power room that the load was ready to be lifted.

Holding his breath, he waited with pounding heart. A few seconds went by, and a slight swaying of the cable told him that the moment had come to begin his aerial journey. He braced his feet as firmly as he could on the projecting rock ledge, and stretched out both his arms. After a short wait he dimly made out the roof of the elevator coming up from the depths. Abruptly he hurled himself forward. His hands grasped a hard, smooth surface, slid down along it for a short distance until they met an obstruction, and then grasped it. At once he found himself hanging in space, surrounded by pitch blackness.

But the plan had not worked out well in every respect. He had misjudged the speed of the machine, and instead of seizing the cross bar his hands had succeeded only in grazing the boards of the dump car on the elevator; they had come to a stop when they reached the lower edge of the platform, which had a kind of flanged rail to which his fingers clung like pincers.

In a second Rejis analyzed his predicament, and in sheer terror realized that it was desperate. Overwhelmed by fright, his hair stood on end and his voice choked in his throat. The shape of that groove allowed him to fit into it only the first two joints of his bent fingers; when he felt, after a few seconds, that they were beginning to slip from the metal because of the heavy pull of his body, all his blood pounded into his heart. Swinging like a pendulum over the abyss, and trembling with anguish and terror, he rent the air with a shrill shout. The terrible intensity of the energy expended by his muscles seemed to fuse his flesh right into the hard iron; and the elevator, dangling beneath it that living appendage, continued its slow, uniform ascent in the vertical shaft.

Some moments sped by in this fashion and Rejis, who felt the blood buzzing in his ears and his heart hammering in his chest, began to estimate the distance travelled. How high was he now? How many yards did he still have to go in order to reach the mouth of the shaft? With his teeth clenched, his face contorted, his eyes starting from their sockets, and his body swept by waves of agony and bathed in cold sweat, each tenth of a second seemed an eternity.

Suddenly, right next to him — almost touching him — the miner caught a fleeting glimpse of something shapeless falling from above like a rock. A brilliant light dazzled him, and he thought he could make out a pale face with two big eyes opened wide, shining in sinister fashion in the darkness. As the two cars passed each other, the sum of their speeds in opposite directions caused a characteristic swishing noise — a noise that resounded in Rejis' brain as if the four archangels of the Apocalypse were shouting to him in chorus: "You are halfway there! There is still a minute to go — that is to say, a century — before the elevator rises the six hundred feet that separate you from the surface, where life — salvation — await you! Each second that passes merely increases the distance your body soon will fall in its dizzy drop to death!"

But he was young and strong, and his whole being, bursting with life, rebelled against this imminent doom. No! He did not want to die! And as the fatal moment kept drawing nearer, his spirit acquired unusual visionary powers: all the events of his lifetime paraded past his eyes in one split second. Understanding that the inevitable was coming closer — that at any instant he was going to let go and fall — he wanted to end the awful agony once and for all. But he remembered the landing that blocked the shaft six hundred and fifty feet below, and a desperate scream of terror broke from his lips. As if he were standing right there, he saw the thick iron plates studded with spikes, rails and bolts, ready to receive the sickening smash of his body hurtling down from seven hundred feet with the speed of a cannon ball.

Suddenly he felt the fingers of his left hand slipping from the hard metal surface, one after another. The elevator went up another sixty feet through the darkness, slowly, silently, invisibly. Then all at once Rejis got the horrible feeling that the fingertips of his right hand were sinking into the iron and going right through it, as if the metal had suddenly melted, and he found himself motionless in space for a fraction of a second. Immediately a mighty crash of thunder boomed inside his brain, and a whirlwind whipped his face, cutting off his breath. . . .

A half minute later, the employes at the mouth of the mine shaft were removing from the extra platform that is sometimes hung from beneath the elevator in order to lower bulky objects into the mine a worker whose hair was streaked with white and whose eyes were wide open in a wild stare, with their pupils enormously dilated. He never recovered his reason, and never learned that while he thought he was dangling over a bottomless abyss there was a thick platform of solid oak just eight inches below his feet.

Ricardo Jaimes Freyre

1872-1933

. . . *Bolivian diplomat, was a professor of history and of literature at the University of Tucumán in northern Argentina. In Buenos Aires he collaborated with his friends Rubén Darío of Nicaragua and Leopoldo Lugones of Argentina in founding the literary publication* Revista de América *(1896). Like his friends, Jaimes Freyre was an exotic Modernist in his poetry. In his volume of verse* Castalia bárbara, *published at the turn of the century, he sought escape in a misty, melancholy Ultima Thule peopled by blond Norse gods.*

This is indeed a far cry from the realities of life in Indian Bolivia atop the Andes. But Señor Jaimes Freyre was also actively engaged in everyday affairs as an educator and a diplomat. He served his government as Minister of Foreign Affairs, and ably represented Bolivia abroad in Rio de Janeiro and in Washington.

His short stories are far from escapist; they often deal with the social problems of his country, whose

*population in the sky-high, windswept altiplano is almost all
pure Indian. The tale translated here treats of the violent reac-
tions of these long-suffering mountain people, a theme developed by several excellent modern novelists of the Andean
countries — Peru, Ecuador and Bolivia. One of the most celebrated is by the Bolivian Alcides Arguedas, whose work* Race
of Bronze *(1919) depicts the bitter life of the Indian in that
stricken land.*

*Jaimes Freyre's short stories anticipated the mainstream of
the contemporary Indianist movement in the literature of the
west coast nations of South America. The background treats of
the archaeological and picturesque elements of native life, but
in the foreground is the note of social protest. Students of
comparative literature who are interested in the theme of the
American Indian should read the prize-winning novel by the
Peruvian Ciro Alegría, whose* Broad and Alien is the World
*(1941) is available in English in a translation by Harriet de
Onís.*

INDIAN JUSTICE

❋ ❋ ❋

T HE TWO TRAVELLERS were having a last drink of wine
as they stood beside the bonfire. The cold morning
breeze made the brims of their broad felt hats flutter
lightly. The fire was growing dim now beneath the pale
white light of dawn, and the farther ends of the broad patio
were becoming slightly more visible. The thick adobe
columns that supported the thatch roof were beginning to
stand out against the shadows in the background.

Tied to a ring that was attached to one of the columns,
two fully saddled horses were waiting with lowered heads,
laboriously chewing long blades of grass. Beside the wall
a young Indian, squatting on his heels, was tossing yellow
grains of corn into his mouth from a full bag he held in
one hand.

When the travellers were ready to leave, two other Indians appeared at the huge, rough-hewn gate. Some thick
beams set into the walls blocked their way; they lifted one
of them and went into the spacious patio. Their humble
and wretched appearance was made even more wretched
and humble by their torn jackets, their coarse shirts left
open at the chest, and the broken and knotted leather
thongs of their sandals.

Slowly they approached the travellers, who were now
mounting their horses, while the Indian guide fastened

45

the bag of corn to his belt and tightly bound the leather thongs of his sandals about his legs. The travellers were still young: one was tall, very fair-complexioned, and had a cold, hard expression; the other was small, dark-complexioned, and had a gay air about him.

"Señor . . . ," mumbled one of the Indians. The white traveller turned toward him.

"Hello! What is it, Tomás?"

"Señor . . . let me have my horse."

"Again, you imbecile! Do you want me to travel on foot? I gave you mine in exchange, and that's enough."

"But your horse is dead."

"Of course he's dead, but that's because I made him run fifteen hours at a stretch. He was a great horse! Yours is worthless. Do you think he'll last many hours?"

"I sold my llama to buy that horse for the fiesta on St. John's Day. Besides, señor, you burned my hut."

"Certainly, because you came bothering me with your whining. I threw a firebrand at your head so you'd go away; you ducked, and the firebrand landed in a pile of straw. It's not my fault: you should have received my firebrand with respect. And you — what do you want, Pedro?" he asked, addressing the other Indian.

"I come to beg you, señor, not to take away my lands. They are mine. I sowed them."

"This is your affair, Córdova," said the rider, turning to his companion.

"No, it certainly is not my affair. I did what I was instructed to do. You don't own those lands, Pedro Quispe. Where are your legal titles — your papers?"

"I have no papers, señor. My father had no papers either, and my father's father didn't know anything about them. And nobody has ever wanted to take our lands

away. You want to give them to somebody else. I haven't
done you any harm."

"Do you have a bagful of coins hidden away somewhere?
Give me the bag and I'll leave you your lands."

Pedro looked at Córdova with anguish in his eyes. "I
have no coins, and I couldn't raise that much money."

"Then there's nothing more to talk about. Leave me
alone."

"In that case, pay me what you owe me."

"Aren't we ever going to get this over with? Do you
think I'm fool enough to pay you for a sheep and some
chickens you gave me? Did you imagine we were simply
going to starve to death?"

The white traveller, who was beginning to grow impatient, exclaimed: "If we keep on listening to these two im-
beciles we'll be here forever."

The top of the mountain against whose slope the big,
rustic lodge nestled was beginning to glow now as the first
rays of sunlight reached it. The barren countryside was
slowly growing light, and the dry, austere landscape, limited by a blackish range of hills nearby, stood out boldly
beneath the blue of a sky overcast by patches of scudding,
lead-bellied clouds.

Córdova signalled the guide, who went toward the gate.
Behind him the two riders started out.

Pedro Quispe hurtled toward them and seized the reins
of one of the horses. A slash with a whip, full in the face,
made him fall back. Then the two Indians left the patio
and ran quickly to a nearby hill. They clambered up with
the speed and sure-footedness of a vicuña, and when they
reached the top looked all about them. Pedro Quispe raised
to his lips the horn he wore hanging down over his shoulders, and blew a long, low note. He paused a moment, and
then continued with quick, shrill blasts.

THE TRAVELLERS were beginning to ascend the slope of the mountain, and the guide, with sure, steady steps, went plodding along stolidly, munching his grains of corn. At the sound of the horn the Indian stopped, looked with alarm at the two riders, and dashed off at top speed along a path that lead into the hills. A few moments later he was lost to view in the distance.

Córdova turned to his companion and said, "Alvarez, those scoundrels have taken our guide away from us. . . ."

Alvarez stopped his horse and looked uneasily in all directions: "The guide . . . and why do we need him? I'm afraid of something worse."

The horn kept sounding, and at the crest of the hill Pedro Quispe stood silhouetted against the blue horizon, atop the barren, reddish ridge. It might be said that a magic spell was being cast over the hills and byways. Behind the huge haystacks, among the fields of coarse wild grass and in the dense underbrush, beneath the broad canvas tents of the mining camps, at the doors of the huts, and along the skyline of the distant hills, figures were seen to appear and disappear in rapid succession. They would stop briefly, direct their gaze toward the hill where Pedro Quispe was rending the air with ceaseless blasts on his horn, and then creep cautiously up the slopes.

Alvarez and Córdova kept riding up the mountain, their horses breathing heavily on the narrow trail through rough, rocky terrain. The two riders, deeply worried, let themselves be carried along in silence. Suddenly an enormous boulder, set loose from the top of the hill, rumbled past them with a roar . . . then another . . . and another. . . .

Alvarez spurred his horse on at top speed, and made him go around behind the hill; Córdova at once did likewise, but boulders kept following them. The whole mountainside seemed to be crumbling down. Driven on madly, the horses jumped over the rocks, miraculously kept their footing on jutting crags, and balanced in space at a dizzy height.

Soon the mountain tops were crowded with Indians. The horsemen then sped toward the narrow ravine beneath them that wound along with a clear, thin thread of water flowing gently through it. The valleys were filled with a strange music as the harsh, unpleasant sound of the horn rose from every side; and at the end of the pass, in the dazzling light that shone between two mountain peaks, a group of men suddenly appeared. At this moment a huge stone struck Alvarez' horse, which teetered briefly, fell, and then went rolling down the mountainside. Córdova dismounted and started to crawl toward the place where the dust-covered horse and rider could be seen.

The Indians began to come down from the heights. Out from the crevices and notches they came, one by one, advancing cautiously and stopping frequently to gaze with watchful eyes at the bottom of the ravine. When they reached the edge of the brook they could see the two travellers. Alvarez, stretched out upon the ground, was motionless. Beside him his companion stood with arms folded in helpless desperation, following intently the slow, fearful descent of the Indians.

ON A NARROW, ROLLING STRETCH of ground, nestled in a hollow formed by hills that flanked its four sides with four wide crests, the old men and the women waited together for the outcome of the manhunt. The Indian women, with their short, round skirts made of coarse fabric, their shawls wrapped about them, their resplendent cloth caps, their coarse braids falling down their backs, stood barefooted in a silent group at one end, as their spools and spindles danced dizzily in their fingers.

When the hunters arrived, they brought the travellers tied across their horses. Advancing to the center of the level space, they dumped the two of them on the ground like bundles of clothing. Then the women drew near and looked at them curiously without interrupting their spinning, and talked in low tones.

The Indians consulted briefly and then one group hastened toward the foot of the mountain. They returned, bringing two large pitchers and two huge poles. And while some dug holes in the ground to set up the poles, others filled small clay cups with liquor from the pitchers. Then they drank until the sun began to sink over the horizon. Nothing could be heard but the sound of the hushed conversation of the women and the gurgle of the liquid poured into the cups as the pitchers were tilted.

Pedro and Tomás took the bodies of the riders and tied them to the posts. Alvarez, whose spine was broken, uttered a long moan. The two Indians stripped them, throwing all their clothing far away, piece by piece. The women stared in amazement at their white bodies.

Then began the torture. Pedro Quispe pulled out Córdova's tongue, and burned his eyes. Tomás, with a knife, covered Alvarez' body with tiny cuts. Then the other Indians came and tore out their hair, stoned them, and put splinters in their wounds. A young Indian girl, laughing, poured a big jar of corn liquor over Alvarez' head.

The afternoon was fading. Long since, the two travellers had yielded up their souls to the Great Judge. And the Indians, tired and surfeited now, kept on beating and hacking the bodies senselessly.

Then it was necessary to swear silence. Pedro Quispe drew a cross on the ground, and the men and women came and kissed it. Then from his neck he took the rosary he always wore, and the Indians swore upon it. He spat upon the ground, and the Indians jumped over the wet earth.

As they disposed of the blood-covered remains and covered up the last traces of the scene that had just taken place upon that wild and desolate plateau, the boundless night was closing in upon the solitude of the sierras.

Ricardo Palma

1833-1919

is Peru's greatest literary figure, and one of the most renowned in all Spanish America. This reputation is based directly upon his short stories, which he called "traditions." They are tales created from a unique and inimitable blend of history, customs, legends, folklore, satire and humor.

As a young man Palma was a poet of the romantic school then in vogue in Latin America. Born in Peru's capital, he attended the University of San Marcos there, but withdrew before graduation to devote himself to politics, journalism and literature. He left Peru only for a brief trip to Europe, where he paid his respects to such romantics as Lamartine and Zorrilla; he also spent a short time in political exile. The rest of his long life he lived in his beloved Lima, as Director of the National Library.

When he was almost forty Palma created the new medium that was to make him famous throughout the Spanish-speaking world — his "traditions." These historical anecdotes, written in a light, charming prose style, were published intermittently in twelve volumes between 1872 and 1918. Although Palma drew his episodes from the rich storehouse of Peru's colorful past — from Inca times to the days of the independent Republic — the Spanish colonial period, particularly in Lima, was his favorite source. It was also the favorite period of his modern readers, for Lima has always been an aristocratic city with strong cultural ties to Old Spain.

Of the three hundred years of Spanish rule, the eighteenth century was the most colorful; Palma painted it with skill and charm. He is the chronicler of colonial Lima. With tongue-in-cheek humor and delicious satire, he writes of every facet of that city's life in those lusty days, and gives us a vast social panorama of the times: amorous Spanish noblemen, lovely and indiscreet ladies, swordsmen, gamblers, clergymen, Creoles, Indians — every human type in the teeming capital of Spain's South American empire. He treats with equal grace and humor such widely divergent eighteenth-century figures as St. Rose of Lima and La Perricholi, the viceroy's mistress. Students of North American literature will recall Thornton Wilder's The Bridge of San Luis Rey, based upon the same period.

The two "traditions" chosen for translation here are representative of his style and subject matter, and are among the favorites of all anthologists. The first is set in the sixteenth century and takes us from the famous silver mining town of Potosí in Upper Peru (now called Bolivia), through El Cuzco, pre-colonial Inca capital, to the "City of Kings," as Lima is called. The second takes place in Lima's seaport, El Callao, and in the eighteenth-century capital itself. The inspiration in this case is simply a phrase used in everyday conversation, for Palma could weave his magic spell out of the thinnest of gossamer threads connecting the present to the past. Both stories stress the great importance attached to personal honor among the peninsular Spaniards during colonial days.

THE MAGISTRATE'S EARS

* * *

IN THE MIDDLE of the sixteenth century, the town of Potosí was the place in the Spanish Empire that attracted a steady stream of adventurers. This explains why, five years after the rich mine had been discovered, its population exceeded twenty thousand souls. The old saying goes

> Mining towns are tough,
> Wide open and rough

and never was a saying more perfectly true than in the case of Potosí during the first two centuries after the Conquest.

The Year of Our Lord 1550 was drawing to a close, and the Chief Magistrate of the town was a lawyer named Don Diego de Esquivel, an ill-tempered and greedy man who, according to all reports, was quite capable of selling justice to the highest bidder in exchange for bars of silver. His Honor was also fond of the fruit of Paradise, and around town there was a good deal of gossip about his amorous escapades. As he had never gotten himself into the predicament where the parish priest had to read him the famous epistle of St. Paul,* Don Diego de Esquivel used to boast of belonging to the brotherhood of bachelors. My personal opinion is that while bachelors may not be exactly a plague on society, they do constitute a threat to the prop-

* St. Paul's Epistle to the Ephesians, especially Chapters v and vi concerning marriage.

erty of their fellow men. It is even held that communists and bachelors are two-legged animals of the same species.

At the moment, His Honor had his eye on a girl from Potosí; but she, who wanted nothing to do with the representative of the law, had very politely refused his advances and placed herself under the protection of a soldier serving with the Tucumán garrison, a handsome young man who was deeply smitten by the young lady's charms. The magistrate, then, was anxiously awaiting an opportunity to take revenge upon the ungrateful girl for her rebuff, and upon the favored young man as well.

As the devil never sleeps, it came about that one night there was a big brawl in one of the many gambling houses that abounded along Quintu Mayu Street in defiance of the ordinances and proclamations of the authorities. One gambler, new at sleight-of-hand and not clever enough to get away with it, had let three dice slip out when a large wager was at stake; some other hothead pulled a knife and pinned his hand to the table top. With all the shouting and hubbub, the night patrol came in, of course, accompanied by the Chief Magistrate carrying his staff of office and a rapier.

"Quiet, everybody! Off to jail with them!" he cried.

The policemen, siding with the gamblers as is usual in such cases, let them all escape through the garret, and limited themselves — for the sake of the record — to nabbing two of the less experienced. Don Diego's joy knew no bounds when he discovered, upon visting the jail next day, that one of the prisoners was his rival, the soldier from the Tucumán garrison.

"Ho, ho, my fine fellow! So you're quite the gambler, too?"

"Well, you see, Your Honor, a nasty toothache had me walking the floor last night, and to see if I could relieve it

I went to that house looking for a countryman of mine who always carries in his money pouch a pair of St. Apolonia's teeth,* which are said to cure that ailment like a charm."

"I'll charm you soon enough, you scoundrel," muttered the judge; and turning to the other prisoner he added, "You gentlemen both know what the law says: one hundred dollars fine, or a dozen lashes. I'll be back at noon, and . . . beware!"

Our soldier's companion sent a message home; the cash for the fine was obtained, and when the magistrate returned he found the full amount ready.

"And you, you rogue; are you going to pay up, or not?"

"I'm as poor as a churchmouse, Your Honor, so you will have to decide what disposition is to be made of my case; for even though they quarter me, they can't get a quarter out of me. I am sorry, but I have nothing to give you."

"Well, a good flogging will do nicely."

"That cannot be, either, Your Honor; for though I am a simple soldier, I am a nobleman from a distinguished family, and my father is one of the twenty-four Aldermen of Seville. Ask my captain, Don Alvaro Castrillón, and Your Lordship will learn that I am as much entitled to use "Don" before my name as the King himself, God save him."

"You a nobleman, Don Knave? Master Antúnez, kindly see that this prince is given a dozen lashes right away."

"Have a care, sir, what you order, for by Heaven, such base treatment is not to be given to a Spanish nobleman!"

"Nobleman? Nobleman? Tell it to me in my other ear!"

"Well, Don Diego," the soldier replied angrily, "if this base and cowardly deed is done, I swear to God and the Virgin Mary that I'll take my revenge on those magistrate's ears of yours!"

* Also, slang for dice.

The lawyer shot a scornful glance at him, and went out for a stroll about the prison courtyard. Shortly afterward Antúnez the jailer, with four of his menials or underlings, brought out the nobleman in shackles, and in the presence of the magistrate dealt him twelve resounding lashes. The victim bore the pain without the slightest sound, and when the whipping was over Antúnez set him free.

"I hold nothing against you, Antúnez," said the victim of the flogging, "but inform the magistrate that from today on those ears of his belong to me; that I am lending them to him for one year; and that he should take care of them as he would my most prized possession."

The jailer guffawed stupidly, and muttered, "This fellow has lost his senses. If he's raving mad, all the lawyer has to do is to hand him over to me, and we'll see if it's true that punishment can make a madman sane."

2

LET US PAUSE, kind reader, and enter the winding corridors of history, for in this series of *Traditions* we have taken it upon ourselves to devote a few lines to the viceroy with whose administration our tale is connected.

After the tragic fate that befell the first viceroy, Don Blasco Núñez de Vela, the Court in Spain thought it unwise to send at once another administrator of such high rank to Peru. Meanwhile a lawyer named La Gasca came to these shores with the title of Governor, invested with sweeping powers and bearing blank orders already signed by Charles V. History tells us that he owed his victory over Gonzalo Pizarro more to shrewdness and skill than to the sword.

Once the country had been pacified, La Gasca himself pointed out to the Emperor the need to name a viceroy

for Peru, and suggested for this post Don Antonio de
Mendoza, Marquis of Mondéjar and Count of Tendilla,
as he was a man experienced in affairs of state and had
already served as viceroy in Mexico.

The Marquis of Mondéjar, second Viceroy of Peru,
entered Lima with little ceremony on the twenty-third of
September of 1551. The country had just been through the
horrors of a long and disastrous war, party passions still
ran high, corruption was widespread, and Francisco Girón
was already preparing to lead the bloody revolution of
1553.

The conditions under which the Marquis of Mondéjar
assumed his powers were certainly inauspicious. He began
by adopting a conciliatory policy and refused (says one
historian) to listen to accusations, which breed reprisals.
It is told of him — adds Lorente — that when a captain
denounced two soldiers for living among the Indians,
feeding themselves by hunting and making gunpower for
their personal use, the Marquis told him with a stern
countenance: "These offenses merit a reward rather than
punishment; if two Spaniards can live among the Indians,
eat what their guns kill, and make gunpowder for their
own use and not to sell, I see nothing criminal about that:
it is rather a great virtue, and an example worthy of imitation. Go with God, and let no one ever come to me again
with such tales, for I don't want to hear them."

Would that rulers would always give such a fine answer
to trouble-making courtiers, professional tattlers, and makers
of revolutions and bombs! The world would be better off.

Though he had an abundance of fine intentions, the
Marquis of Mondéjar succeeded in accomplishing very
little. He directed his son, Don Francisco, to visit El Cuzco,
Chucuito, Potosí and Arequipa, and to draw up a report
about the needs of the Indians; he commissioned Juan
Betanzos to write a history of the Incas; he created the

Halbardier Guards; he issued some wise regulations concerning the policing of the city of Lima; and he severely punished duellists and their seconds. Duels, even for ridiculous reasons, were the fashion of the day, and in many such encounters the opponents would wear blood-red tunics.

The good Don Antonio de Mendoza planned to institute beneficial reforms. Unfortunately his ailments sapped the strength of his spirit, and death carried him off in July of 1552 before he had been in office ten months. A week before his death, on the twenty-first of July, there was heard in Lima a frightful thunderclap accompanied by flashes of lightning, the first time such a thing had happened since the founding of the city.

3

THE FOLLOWING DAY Don Cristóbal de Agüero (for such was the soldier's name) appeared before the captain of the Tucumán troops, Don Alvaro Castrillón, and said to him: "Captain, I beg you, sir, to permit me to resign from the service. His Majesty wants soldiers with honor, and I have lost mine."

Don Alvaro, who had high regard for Aguero, addressed a few remarks to him, but they were of no avail against the soldier's unyielding determination. The captain finally granted his request.

The humiliation inflicted upon Don Cristóbal had remained a secret, for the magistrate had forbidden the jailers to speak of the flogging. Perhaps conscience cried out to Don Diego that he had used his authority as a judge to take revenge upon the gambler for his rebuff as a suitor.

And so three months went by. Then Don Diego received documents calling him to Lima to take possession of an inheritance. Having obtained leave from the local authorities, he began to make arrangements for his journey. He was strolling through Cantumarca on the eve of his departure when a man muffled up in a cloak approached him and asked, "The trip is tomorrow, señor?"

"Is that any busines of yours, you impertinent fellow?"

"Is it any business of mine? It certainly is, since I have to watch out for those ears!" And the muffled man vanished down an alley, leaving Esquivel floundering in a sea of speculation.

In the early morning he began his journey to El Cuzco. On the day he reached the city of the Incas he went out to visit a friend, and upon turning a corner he felt a hand upon his shoulder. Don Diego turned around in surprise, and found his victim from Potosí.

"Don't be frightened, señor. I see that those ears are still in their proper place, and I am glad of it."

Don Diego stood there petrified.

Three weeks later our traveller reached Guamanga, and by nightfall had just installed himself at the inn when there was a knock at the door.

"Who is it?" asked the magistrate.

"Praised be the All Highest," was the reply from outside.

"For ever and ever, amen." And Don Diego went to the door and opened it.

Neither the ghost of Banquo at Macbeth's banquet nor the statue of the Comendador at the home of the libertine Don Juan caused greater astonishment than that felt by the magistrate when he found himself unexpectedly in the presence of the man he had ordered flogged in Potosí.

"Calm yourself, señor. Those ears are still all right? Well then, until we meet again!"

Terror and remorse struck Don Diego speechless.

Finally he reached Lima, and the first time he went out he met our human phantom, who now spoke no word to him, but simply cast an eloquent glance at his ears. There was no way of avoiding him: in church and out walking he stuck to him like a shadow, and was an endless nightmare. Esquivel's nerves were constantly on edge, and the slightest sound made him jump. Neither the inheritance, nor the attention that Lima society — from the viceroy down — showered upon him, nor the banquets, nothing, absolutely nothing could calm his fears. Before his eyes there was always the relentless pursuer. And so the anniversary of the scene at the jail arrived.

It was ten o'clock at night, and Don Diego, having made certain the doors of his room were locked tight, was ensconced in a leather armchair and was writing his correspondence by the light of a dim lamp. Suddenly a man slipped silently through the window of the adjoining room. Two sinewy arms grasped Esquivel, a gag stifled his cries, and strong ropes bound his body to the chair. The nobleman from Postosí stood before him, and a sharp dagger shone in his hand.

"Your Honor," he said to him, "today the year is up; I have come to reclaim my honor."

And with savage serenity he sliced off the ears of the luckless magistrate.

4

DON CRISTÓBAL DE AGÜERO eluded the pursuit of the viceroy, the Marquis of Mondéjar, and succeeded in reaching Spain. He sought an audience with Charles V, asked him to be the judge of his case, and won not only his sovereign's pardon but also a captain's commission in a regiment that was being organized for service in Mexico.

The lawyer died a month later, not so much from the effects of his wounds as from the humiliation of being called "the man who lost his honor with his ears."

MARGARITA'S NIGHTGOWN

* * *

IN ALL PROBABILITY, some of my readers have heard old ladies of Lima say, when they want to emphasize the high price of some article, "Why, this is more expensive than the nightgown of Margarita Pareja!"

I should never have satisfied my curiosity concerning the identity of that Margarita whose gown has become a byword had I not run across an article in the Madrid magazine *La América* written by Don Ildefonso Antonio Bermejo, author of a remarkable book about Paraguay. Although he mentions the young lady and her nightgown merely in passing, he set me to unravelling the threads of the mystery, and I succeeded in bringing to light the story you are about to read.

I

IN THE YEAR 1765 or thereabouts, Margarita Pareja was the most cherished daughter of Don Raimundo Pareja, Knight of the Order of Santiago and Collector of Revenue for the port of Callao. She was one of those lovely ladies of Lima who are so beautiful they captivate the Devil himself, and cause him to make the sign of the Cross and hurl stones madly. She had a pair of dark eyes that were like two torpedoes loaded with dynamite, which used to pierce and shatter the hearts of the swains of Lima.

At about this time there arrived from the Royal City of Madrid an arrogant young Spaniard named Don Luis Alcázar. He had an uncle in Lima, a wealthy bachelor of ancient Aragonese ancestry, who was prouder than the sons of King Fruela.* Of course, until the time came to inherit his uncle's estate our Don Luis was as poor as a church-mouse and lived in dire poverty. When I say that even his escapades were on credit, to be paid for when his fortunes improved, I think I've said quite enough.

At the procession of St. Rose of Lima, Alcázar met the lovely Margarita. The young lady caught his eye and torpedoed his heart. He paid her polite compliments, and though she didn't say yes or no, she indicated with little smiles and other weapons of the feminine arsenal that the young man was very much to her liking. The truth — just as surely as I tell it to my confessor — is that they fell head over heels in love.

Since sweethearts forget the existence of arithmetic, Don Luis thought that his present poverty would be no obstacle to success in love, so he went to Margarita's father and without beating about the bush asked him for his daughter's hand. Don Raimundo did not take kindly to the request, and he courteously dismissed the suitor, telling him that Margarita was as yet too young to have a husband, since in spite of her eighteen years she still played with dolls.

But this was not the real reason. His negative stemmed from the fact that Don Raimundo did not wish to be the father-in-law of a penniless young man. He must have mentioned this confidentially to his friends: one of them went with the story to Don Honorato, for such was the

* An eighth-century king of Asturias, cradle of Spanish nobility and royalty.

name of the Aragonese uncle. The latter, who was haughtier than the Cid, snorted with rage and said: "Well, of all things! Rebuff my nephew? Many men would be tickled just to get him into the family, for there is no finer young man in all Lima. What consummate insolence! How far does that petty little tax collector think he con go with me?"

Margarita, who was well ahead of her century (for she was as nervous as a girl of today), wailed, tore her hair, and went into a swoon; and if she didn't threaten to poison herself it was only because phosphorous matches had not yet been invented. Margarita kept growing paler and losing weight, and was visibly pining away. She talked of becoming a nun, and lost all control over herself. "I'll be the bride of Luis, or of God!" she would scream each time her nerves became upset — which happened once every hour.

The Knight of Santiago became alarmed, and called in physicians and healers. All of them declared that the girl was on the verge of consumption, and that the only remedy that could save her was not sold in the drugstore. Either marry her to the man of her choice, or lay her out in her coffin with a palm leaf and a wreath: such was the medical ultimatum.

Don Raimundo — who was, after all, a father! — forgetting his cloak and cane, dashed madly to the home of Don Honorato and said to him:

"I've come to obtain your consent to your nephew's marriage right away — tomorrow — to Margarita; otherwise we are going to lose the girl very soon."

"It's impossible," answered the uncle caustically. "My nephew is a penniless young man; what you should seek for your daughter is a man who is rolling in wealth."

The interview was stormy. The more Don Raimundo

begged, the more obstinate the Aragonese became. The father was just about to leave in despair when Don Luis, taking a hand in the discussion, said:

"But uncle, it is not Christian for us to cause the death of someone who is not at fault."

"Are you perfectly willing?"

"With all my heart, dear uncle."

"Well then, young man, I consent in order to please you, but with one condition, which is this: Don Raimundo is to swear to me before the consecrated Host that he will not give his daughter a cent, nor leave her a nickel as an inheritance."

Here a new and more volent argument began.

"But, sir," Don Raimundo argued, "my daughter has a dowry of twenty thousand dollars."

"We renounce the dowry. The girl will come to her husband's house with just what she is wearing now."

"Let me give her at least the furniture and her trousseau."

"Not one pin. If you don't agree, we'll drop the matter and the girl can die."

"Be reasonable, Don Honorato. My daughter needs to bring at least a nightgown to replace the one she has on."

"All right; I'll make an exception of that garment so you won't accuse me of being stubborn. I consent to your giving Margarita her bridal nightgown, and that's all!"

The following day Don Raimundo and Don Honorato went early in the morning to the Church of San Francisco. They knelt to hear mass, and according to their agreement, at the moment the priest raised the Host, Margarita's father said: "I swear not to give my daughter more than her bridal nightgown. May God condemn me if I fail to keep my oath."

2

AND DON RAIMUNDO PAREJA kept his oath *ad pedem litterae:* neither in life nor in death did he ever give his daughter another thing of the slightest value.

The Belgian lace that adorned the bride's nightgown cost two thousand seven hundred dollars, according to the statement of Bermejo, who apparently took this bit of information from the *Noticias secretas* of Ulloa and Don Jorge Juan.* Furthermore, the drawstring at the neck consisted of a little chain of diamonds valued at thirty thousand dollars.

The newlyweds let the Aragonese uncle think that the gown was worth only a few dollars at most, for Don Honorato was so pig-headed that had he learned the truth he would have forced his nephew to get a divorce.

Let us agree that the fame achieved by the bridal nightgown of Margarita Pareja was indeed deserved.

* Jorge Juan and Antonio Ulloa were in Peru in the eighteenth century as members of a scientific expedition. They were instructed by the king to make a secret report to him on conditions in America.

Hector Velarde

1898-

is, like Ricardo Palma, a commentator on the Lima scene. Unlike his compatriot, however, who preferred the colonial period, Velarde concentrates on the Peruvian capital in the twentieth century. His particular forte is life in the growing middle and professional class, to which he himself — an engineer — belongs.

Velarde is a cultured cosmopolitan: his mother was of German extraction, and he received a French education. Perhaps this international outlook helps him to stand back and view the contemporary scene with detached good humor; his thumbnail sketches of the foibles of Lima society are filled with subtle irony. Indeed, Velarde is one of the very few humorous writers in all Spanish America today, where the belief apparently prevails that literature should be exclusively a serious matter.

In the selection translated here (the title in the original story is in English — "Father's Day") Velarde pokes good-humored fun at the typical *tourist-in-a-hurry who knows no language but English and has little understanding of another culture — a stereotype all too tragically true. But even as he has fun at the expense of the English Protestant clergyman, Velarde satirizes the social conditions in the Peruvian capital. There are still some slum districts in Lima (as in every big city in the world) but the swarms of beggars and sharpers no longer ply their picaresque professions. Much social progress has been made since this story was written some years ago. Lottery tickets, however, are still in abundant evidence in almost every Spanish American country.*

FATHER'S DAY

* * *

YESTERDAY I WENT to meet Harry Potter, nephew of old Mr. Potter, that Englishman who was so rich he died of an attack of indigestion in Lima's Central Market. Do you remember the newspapers mentioned him . . . he resigned from the Municipal Council . . . ?

No, I don't remember.

Well, no matter; I knew him well. I felt duty bound to welcome his nephew, Harry, at Callao, and show him around Lima.

Harry knew me only by name. I found he was a Protestant pastor, a very serious, pleasant man with glasses, who spoke only English. All this by means of a little English-Spanish Spanish-English dictionary that I carried in my coat pocket.

I discovered that Harry was very methodical. He said to me:

"I am very much interested in getting to know your lovely city; my ship leaves early tomorrow for Valparaiso; it is now two o'clock in the afternoon; here is my list."

I read: First, go to the bank. Second, buy fruit. Third, go to the Gran Hotel Bolívar where a friend of mine, Miss Coolingham, is staying. Fourth, get a haircut. Fifth, visit the Lima cemetery where my uncle is buried. Sixth, see a little of the town. Seventh, go to a church to thank God for the good crossing I had from Liverpool. Eighth, eat in some inexpensive restaurant. Ninth, get back on board the ship.

"Very well," I told Potter; and I popped him into my Chevrolet. I sped him to Lima like a shot, without giving him much chance to see anything along the road.

"What's that?" he asked me as we swept along.

"Those are low Inca walls," I answered. They were just adobe fences around some pasture lands.

Suddenly I dumped him in front of the National City Bank. Potter had no time to finish saying the word "beautiful" because a mulatto boy selling lottery tickets shoved one under his nose:

"It's number 13, mister!"

Potter took the ticket, rolled it up into a little ball, and threw it into the street.

While the seller was looking for the crumpled ticket, making rather impolite references to Potter's family, Potter couldn't get into the bank because his way was blocked by an unkempt woman carrying a dozing baby in her arms.

"Mister, please mister, this nice number. . . ."

Potter stood looking for a moment at the lottery ticket the woman was offering him, and then whizzed into the bank like a comet.

As Potter was conscientiously inspecting and signing a stack of bank drafts and travellers' checks, he began to feel a slight tug at his jacket. He turned around and discovered a wretched little Indian girl, with hardly a stitch of clothing on her, saying in a pitiful voice:

"Please, mister, buy this little ticket I'm selling; give me a penny, mister; my poor mother. . . ."

Potter made a gesture of impatience when he saw that the little girl had slipped a series of lottery tickets in among his drafts and checks.

"What's this?" he asked me in alarm.

I took out my pocket dictionary and looked up the word *suerte*.

"Luck," I said.

"Ah!" he exclaimed, "good luck!" He patted the Indian girl's cheek, carefully returned her tickets, and gave her a little religious print he took out of his Bible.

When Potter left the bank, the mulatto boy, the unkempt woman, and a partially crippled man rushed up to him and shouted:

"Here it is, mister! Twenty thousand dollars! (Dirty gringo!) For today's drawing! Don't turn me down, please, boss? Gimme a dime!"

Almost running, we reached the car. Potter showed me his list. I explained that it would be better to go to the cemetery right from there, and we drove down Maravillas Street.

Just as we were pulling up to the cemetery gate, a horde of tattered kids carrying stepladders and rags raced up and swarmed all over the Chevrolet. Climbing on the running boards, hanging on to the door handles, endangering their lives, they shouted as they stuck their heads in the windows:

"Can I clean off the tombstone, mister? I cleaned it for you yesterday! Wipe your car, mister? I'm the one you know! Hey, doc! I was first! I'll take off the gasoline cap for you! Let me take care of the flowers! Me, mister, me . . . !"

Potter, smiling and waving at them with a kind of benevolent superiority, looked at me and asked as he pointed to the cemetery gate, "Circus?"

He thought a circus performance had been arranged there, and that they had taken him for the clown.

When he left the car a cloud of dust enveloped Potter, who was having a hard time in the midst of stepladders, rags, stools, and sprays of flowers. I had to intervene forcibly, but I couldn't prevent the boys from following him to the niche where his uncle lay buried. From a distance, while Potter was praying, the boys kept attracting his attention discreetly with subdued sounds of "Psst!" while they pointed to cloths for wiping off the burial plaque and stepladders for climbing up.

When we got back we saw that other boys were rubbing the Chevrolet energetically, and were trying hard to get the car doors open so we could climb in.

"I wiped it off for you, mister! I'm the one with the green rag! Here I am, mister . . . me!"

One of them, excessively courteous, closed the door for Potter and mashed one of his fingers.

Potter, after examining his finger closely, said to me, "The nail."

I took out my little dictionary. It meant *la uña*.

In order to get started I threw a quarter quite a distance away. There was a violent scramble of boys and dirt, and we got away quickly.

When we reached Santa Ana Street I discovered that they had stolen the cap from my gas tank.

We stopped in the Plaza de Armas, where a deaf-mute came up to us. He was fat and ruddy-faced, and wore a cap. He whistled three times, uttered a series of guttural sounds, and made gestures to Potter outlining the recent construction of the rounded arcades. Potter said to him gravely, "Sorry, I am English."

We looked at the list, and I suggested to Potter that we go to a barber shop nearby. He explained to me that the barber aboard his ship had stayed in Panama with a Malayan dancing girl.

While we were going through the arcade, some dirty kids followed Potter, shouting their wares at him:

"Five mothballs for a dime! Incense papers? Balloon, mister? Take home this toy mouse for your little boy!"

Potter murmured, "How interesting, how interesting. . . ."

No sooner had we entered the shop than a Japanese barber shouted, as if calling out orders in a cheap restaurant, "Shave, haircut, shampoo, and a shoeshine!"

"Just a haircut," I told him.

They sat Potter down, threw a sheet over him, and gave him an Argentine magazine. A shirtless little Negro boy shined his shoes and stopped whistling from time to time to offer him a lottery ticket. Meanwhile they gave him such a close haircut that he looked like a Buddhist priest. Potter came out of the barber shop slightly nonplussed.

"And now?" I asked him.

"Church," he told me.

I accompanied him to the Church of Santo Domingo. There, something unusual was going on — a ceremony, surely. A mass of beggars of both sexes and of all races and ages pounced on Potter, and he tripped over a legless man who was on the floor. Two girls wearing ribbons were standing at the door rattling coin-filled canisters which they shoved at him as two other girls pinned tiny yellow rosettes on his lapel.

"And this?" asked Potter.

"It's Father's Day," I said, just give him some answer.

When Potter was in the middle of his prayers, two bare-footed little Indian girls, one very alert and the other blind, tapped him on the back and held out their hands. Potter changed his pew. He sat down next to an old lady dressed outlandishly. She smelled bad. Potter changed to another pew, and a dog came out from under the bench where it had been sleeping.

As we went out Potter, surrounded by all the beggars, kept scratching himself in alarm, with the expression of a man who thinks he has caught some strange disease. I took out my pocket dictionary, looked up *pulga*, and said to him: "Fleas, fleas. . . ."

"Oh," exclaimed Potter. "Thank you very much."

"What else?" I asked him.

He looked at his list and said, "Fruit."

I took him to Giaccoletti's. We had to leave the car near the Metro movie theater, where it was welcomed with joy.

"Wipe your car, mister? I wiped it for you this morning! Me, professor! I'm the fellow who did it last night!"

Potter was struck by the cheerfulness and persistence of these boys.

Outside Giaccoletti's a tall, snowy-haired man with white sneakers came up to him, bowed ceremoniously, and offered him a lottery ticket. At the same time two little Indian girls tugged at his trousers and asked him for a nickel. I took Potter by the arm and led him inside the store, where there was a crowd of people standing. While we were picking out the fruit and Potter was enjoying a snack of meat pie, a little mulatto with a skin disease and wearing just an undershirt got tangled up in his legs. Potter took out his handkerchief and blew his nose.

"We had better go," I told him. "According to your list you still have to visit Miss Coolingham at the Hotel Bolívar."

"No," Potter answered. "Dinner."

"How early these gringos eat!" I thought. And I took him to Raimondi's.

There, slouching in doorways or sitting on the curbstone, were some beggars with their children. They rushed at Potter, some with lottery tickets, others with dented tin cups, still others showing him their birth defects. . . .

Potter felt the fleas he had picked up in the church

launching a new offensive. Scratching himself, and displaying his Japanese haircut, he went into the restaurant, which was jammed. We found a seat as best we could, and ordered soup. While Potter was eating his, a quiet little mulatto girl pushed a lottery ticket near his plate. Potter remained unmoved. The girl kept moving it nearer and nearer to him, obviously hoping he would eat it.

"How formal these English are!" I thought to myself. "A lottery ticket is practically put into their soup, and they don't utter a word!"

After some roast beef and some stewed pears we left, followed by the quiet little mulatto girl. We were set upon by the beggars outside, whose number and activity had increased. I felt somewhat ashamed, but Potter smiled as though it were a quaint custom on a local holiday.

The only remaining item on his list was to visit Miss Coolingham. We went to the Bolívar. Next to the drugstore a man without a collar, but wearing a top hat, asked Potter if he could let him have a pair of old shoes. Potter went upstairs and I stayed in the lobby of the hotel talking in English to a lady from the town of Piura. In a short time Potter came down and said to me:

"Miss Coolingham has five lottery tickets and wants the desk to send up this afternoon's newspaper. . . ."

We took care of this for Miss Coolingham, and went out the side door. Night had fallen. Waiting for us were three women draped in black shawls — mysterious and forbidding, with a studied air of tragedy — who approached like shades, stretched out their grasping, ghostly hands from beneath a mass of rags, and murmured into Potter's ear:

"I have fourteen hungry little children . . . My husband died last night in the hospital and I have no money to bury him. . . ."

"I have a young daughter, quite grown-up, very attractive. . . ."

Potter and I quickened our pace. We jumped into the Chevrolet and shot off toward Callao. During the ride Potter said to me:

"What an interesting day your Father's Day is! And what a nice custom you have — opening up all the asylums, hospitals, orphanages and reform schools in the country so that the poor wretches may go out and do what they want on this day. It's a really humane idea!"

"Er . . . yes," I murmured.

When we reached the dock area a dozen kids came running to give us a magnificent reception.

"Wipe your car, mister? I'm the one! Me!"

Potter took a handful of coins from his pocket and threw them in the air with a triumphant gesture, exclaiming: "Father's Day! Father's Day! Good-bye!"

Before saying good-bye to me and going up the gangplank, Potter asked me confidentially, "What are those little tickets they call *huachitos?*"

"Bonds of God," I answered.

Then he embraced me and said, "How fortunate your country is to have so many holders of shares in Heaven!"

And Potter, with a Japanese haircut and full of fleas, boarded his ship and went below.

Leopoldo Lugones

1874-1938

*most famous of the Argentine Modernists, was —
like his friend Rubén Darío — a poet and short
story writer. He was also active in public life as Director of the National Council on Education, and
represented Argentina as a member of the Com-
mittee on Intellectual Cooperation of the League
of Nations, more or less the equivalent of UNESCO
in the United Nations today.*

*Lugones' life was a constant inner struggle: he
was at war with the world and with himself. Starting out as an anarchist and then a zealous international Socialist, he passed through the political and
intellectual wringer until he came out an ardent
Catholic nationalist. And in his literary ideology he
went from a kind of neo-gongorism through roman-
ticism and symbolism to realism. Hopelessly embit-
tered, he finally committed suicide.*

*Lugones' writing was a constant striving for new
ways to express his inner turmoil. His earlier van-
guardist, Modernist poetry, inspired by the French*

symbolists, gave way in his later years to verse based on a return to the primitive Spanish poets. And in his short stories the almost baroque style of his youthful works became much more simplified in later collections.

In the stories written early in the twentieth century, particularly in the volume entitled Las fuerzas extrañas (Strange Forces), we find elements of fantasy, tragedy, and abnormality. The tale we have translated here comes from this group, which is perhaps his most celebrated. Edgar Allan Poe is his North American counterpart in this collection. The idea that apes really "descended" from men is certainly a novel one, and Lugones develops it with full pseudo-scientific irony.

YZUR

*　*　*

I BOUGHT THE MONKEY at the auction sale of a circus that had gone bankrupt.

The first time it occurred to me to try the experiment described in these lines was one afternoon as I was reading in some article or other that the natives of Java used to attribute the lack of speech in monkeys not to the fact that they cannot talk, but simply that they will not. "They refrain from speech," it said, "so that people will not put them to work."

This idea, which I did not take seriously at first, came to engross me until it evolved into this anthropological theory: monkeys were men who for some reason or other stopped speaking. This caused the vocal organs and the brain centers that control speech to atrophy to the point where the relationship between the two grew so weak that it virtually disappeared. The language of the species was reduced to inarticulate cries, and the primitive human sank to animal level.

It is obvious that if this could be demonstrated, all the strange characteristics that make monkeys such unusual creatures would be readily explained. But there could be only one possible proof of this: to get a monkey to talk again.

Meanwhile I had travelled all over the world with my monkey, drawing him closer and closer to me through our wanderings and adventures. In Europe he attracted everyone's attention, and had I wanted to I could have made him as much a celebrity as Consul;* but my status as a business man was out of keeping with such foolishness.

Inspired by my firm convictions about speech in monkeys, I went through the entire bibliography on the subject without any appreciable result. The only thing I knew with absolute certainty was that *there is no scientific reason why a monkey cannot speak.* This took five years of study and thought.

Yzur — where he got this name I never could find out, since his former owner did not know either — Yzur was certainly a remarkable animal. The training he received in the circus, although limited almost entirely to mimicry, had greatly developed his faculties; this was what impelled me even more to try out my apparently absurd theory upon him. Moreover, it is known that the chimpanzee (which Yzur was) is one of the most docile of monkeys and the best equipped mentally, which increased my chances of success. Every time I saw him walking along on two feet with his hands behind his back to keep his balance, cutting a figure like a drunken sailor, the conviction that he was a retarded human grew stronger in me.

Actually, there is no reason why a monkey should not form words with precision. His natural speech, that is to say the combination of cries by which he communicates with his fellow creatures, is quite diversified; his larynx, although different from a human being's, does not differ as much as a parrot's does — yet parrots can speak; and as for his brain, in addition to the fact that comparison with that of a parrot dispels all doubt, it should be recalled that an idiot's brain is also undeveloped — and in spite of this, there are idiots who can pronounce some words. As far as Broca's convolution is concerned, this depends, of course, upon the total development of the brain; moreover, it has

* Consul, the Almost-Human, a nineteenth-century hoax.

not been proved conclusively that this is the area that controls speech. Although it is the most likely area anatomically, there are, nevertheless, incontrovertible arguments to the contrary.

Happily, a monkey has — added to his many bad characteristics — a love of learning, as his flair for imitation reveals: good memory, powers of reflection developed even to the point of skillful pretending, and an attention span better developed, comparatively, than that of a child. He is, then, a pedagogical subject of the most promising type.

Moreover, mine was young, and it is known that youth is a monkey's most intelligent period. The only difficulty lay in the method I should use to teach him words. I was acquainted with all the unfruitful attempts of my predecessors, and it goes without saying that in view of the competence of some of them and the completely negative results of all their efforts, my determination faltered on more than one occasion. But all my thoughts on the subject kept drawing me to this conclusion: *the first step is to develop the monkey's organs of sound production.*

This is, indeed, the way one proceeds with deaf-mutes before getting them to articulate. And scarcely had I begun to think about this, when analogies between monkeys and deaf-mutes came abundantly to mind. First of all, there is their extraordinary facility for imitation, which compensates for articulated speech and shows that failure to speak does not mean failure to think, even though there may be a lessening of this latter faculty due to the paralysis of the former. Then there are other characteristics, more peculiar because they are more specific: diligence in work, fidelity, and courage, which are increased certainly by two factors whose interrelation is surely revealing — a knack for balancing tricks, and resistance to dizziness.

I decided, then, to begin my work with practical lip and tongue exercises for my monkey, thus treating him like a deaf-mute. After that, his hearing would help me to establish direct verbal communication without the need for recourse to the sense of touch. The reader will note that in this I was planning ahead too optimistically.

Fortunately, among all the great apes the chimpanzee has the most mobile lips, and in this particular case Yzur, who had suffered from sore throats, knew how to open his mouth wide so they could examine it. The first inspection confirmed — in part — my suspicions: his tongue lay at the bottom of his mouth like an inert mass, motionless except when swallowing. The exercises soon had their effect, for after two months he knew how to stick out his tongue to sass me. This was the first connection he made between moving his tongue and an idea — a relationship, moreover, quite in keeping with his make-up.

The lips caused greater trouble: it was even necessary to stretch them with tweezers. But he appreciated — perhaps by my expression — the importance of that strange task, and set about it with a will. While I practiced the movements for him to imitate, he would sit there with his arm twisted behind him scratching his rump, and blinking in quizzical concentration; or else he would stroke his hairy cheeks with the air of a man who is marshalling his thoughts by helping them along with rhythmic gestures. At last he learned how to move his lips.

But language skills are not easily mastered, as is shown by a child's long period of prattling, which leads him into the acquisition of speech habits only as his intellect develops. Indeed, it has been shown that the center of voice production is associated with the speech center of the brain in such a way that their normal development depends upon their working in tandem. This had already been foreseen as a logical deduction in 1785 by Heinicke, inventor of the oral method of teaching deaf-mutes. He used to speak of the "dynamic concatenation of ideas," a phrase so crystal clear that it would do honor to more than one contemporary psychologist.

As for language arts, Yzur was in the same situation as a child who understands many words before beginning to speak; but he was much more adept at forming proper decisions about things because of his greater experience with life. These decisions must have been the result not only of impressions but also of intellectual curiosity and investigation, to judge by their varied character. Since this presupposes abstract reasoning, it revealed in him a high degree of intelligence, which was certainly very helpful for my purpose.

If my theories seem too bold, it should be borne in mind that the syllogism, which is the basis of logical reasoning, is not alien to the mind of many animals. This is true because the syllogism is basically a comparison between two sensations; if not, why do animals who know man flee from him, while those who never knew him do not?

I began, then, the phonetic education of Yzur. It was a question of teaching him first the mechanics of speech, and then leading him gradually into speaking meaningfully. The monkey had this much of an advantage over a deaf-mute: he possessed a voice, and had better control over his organs of articulation. It was a question of teaching him how to modulate his voice, that is, how to pronounce sounds, which teachers call static if they are vowels and dynamic if they are consonants.

In view of a monkey's fondness for food — and following in this instance a method employed by Heinicke with deaf-mutes — I decided to associate each vowel with something good to eat: *a* with *potato*, *e* with *beet*, *i* with *pie*, *o* with *cocoa,* and *u* with *prune,* working things out so that the vowel should be contained in the name of the tidbit, either alone and repeated, as in *cocoa,* or combining the basic sounds in both stressed and unstressed syllables, as in *potato.* All went well as far as the vowels were concerned, that is, sounds formed with the mouth open. Yzur learned them in two weeks. The *u* was the hardest for him to pronounce.

The consonants gave me a devilish amount of work. I soon came to the conclusion that he would never succeed in pronouncing those formed by using both the teeth and gums: his long eye teeth completely prevented this. His vocabulary was limited, then, to the five vowels plus *b, k, m, g, f* and *c,* that is, all the consonants formed by using only the palate and the tongue. Even for this, the aural method was not enough; I had to resort to the sense of touch as with a deaf-mute, resting his hand on my chest and then on his own so that he could feel the sound vibrations.

And so three years went by, without getting him to form a single word. He tended to name things after the letter that predominated in them. That was all.

In the circus he had learned to bark like a dog, for they were his working companions; and when he saw me lose hope in the face of my vain attempts to elicit speech from him, he would bark loudly as if he were showing me all he knew. He would pronounce the vowels and consonants separately, but he was unable to combine them. At most he would come out with a giddy succession of p's and m's.

Despite the slow progress, a great change had come over his character. He moved his features less, his expression was more intelligent, and he struck thoughtful poses. He had acquired, for example, the habit of staring at the stars.

His sensitivity had likewise increased: he was more in-clined to cry easily.

The lessons continued with unyielding determination, although with no greater success. The whole business had become a painful obsession, and little by little I felt inclined to use force. My dispositon was becoming more bitter with failure, until it reached the point of unconscious hostility toward Yzur.

He was becoming more moody in his deep, stubborn silence, and was beginning to convince me that I would never get him out of it, when suddenly I realized that he wasn't speaking because he didn't want to!

The cook came in horror to tell me one evening that he had surprised the monkey "speaking real words." According to his story, Yzur was squatting next to a fig tree in the garden; but terror prevented the cook from recalling the heart of the matter, that is, the words themselves. He thought he could remember only two: *bed* and *pipe*. I almost kicked him for his stupidity.

Needless to say, I spent the night in the grip of great emotion. And what I hadn't done for three years — the error that ruined everything—came as the result of the irritability brought on by that sleepless night, and by excessive curiosity as well.

Instead of letting the monkey come to the point of showing his command of speech naturally, I summoned him the next day and tried to get it out of him by making him obey me. All I got was the p's and m's with which I was fed up, the hypocritical winks, and — may Heaven forgive me — a certain hint of ridicule in the restless mo-bility of his grimaces. I became angry, and without think-ing I whipped him. The only result was tears, and an absolute silence unbroken even by moaning.

Three days later he fell ill with a kind of mental depression complicated by symptoms of meningitis. Leeches, cold showers, purgatives, counterirritants, alcoholatures, bromides — every remedy for the terrible illness was given to him. With determination born of desperation I struggled on, driven by remorse and fear, the former because I believed the animal to be a victim of my cruelty, the latter because I feared for the secret he was carrying, perhaps, to the grave.

He improved after a great while, but was so weak, however, that he could not stir from his bed. The nearness of death had ennobled and humanized him: his eyes, full of gratitude, were never off me, and followed me all around the room like two rotating globes even though I went behind him; his hand sought mine in the companionship of convalescence. In my great solitude, he was rapidly acquiring the status of a person.

Nonetheless, the demon of investigation, which is nothing but the spirit of perversity, drove me to renew my experiments. The monkey had really talked. I just couldn't leave it at that.

I began very slowly, asking him for the letters he knew how to pronounce. Not a sound! I left him alone for hours and watched him through a little hole in the partition. Not a sound! I spoke to him in short sentences, trying to play upon his faithfulness or his liking for food. Not a sound! When my sentences were sad, his eyes would fill with tears. When I used a familiar sentence such as "I am your master," with which I used to begin all my lessons, or "You are my monkey," with which I used to follow up my first statement in order to convey to his mind the finality of a complete truth, he would denote agreement by closing his eyelids. But he would not utter a sound, not even go so far as to move his lips.

He had gone back to signs as his only means of communicating with me, and this fact, coupled with his points of similarity with deaf-mutes, caused me to redouble my precautions, since everyone knows how very prone deaf-mutes are to mental illness. At times I wanted him to lose his mind to see if delirium would finally break his silence.

His convalescence was not progressing: the same emaciation, the same sadness. It was obvious that he was mentally and emotionally ill; his whole constitution had been undermined by some malfunction of the brain, and sooner or later his case would be hopeless. But in spite of the increasing submissiveness caused by the disease, his silence — that maddening silence brought on by my desperate action — continued unbroken. From some dim background of tradition which had become instinct, the species was imposing its millennial silence upon the animal, whose ancestral will was strengthened by his own inner being. The primitive men of the jungle who had been forced into silence — that is, into intellectual suicide — by some unknown and barbaric injustice, were keeping their secret; forest mysteries dating from the dawn of history still held sway across the enormous gulf of time in his now unconscious decision.

The great families of four-handed anthropoids, unfortunately retarded in the course of evolution and surpassed by man, who oppressed them with brutal barbarism, had doubtless been dethroned and had lost their sway in the leafy realm of their primitive Eden. Their ranks had been decimated, and their females had been captured so that organized slavery might begin with the mother's womb. In their helpless, conquered state they had been impelled to express their human dignity by breaking the unhappy but higher bond — speech — that linked them to their enemies, and as a final safeguard they had taken refuge in the obscurity of the animal kingdom.

And what horrors, what monstrous excesses of cruelty must the conquerors have committed upon these half-beasts during the course of their evolution to cause them — after having known intellectual pleasure, the forbidden fruit of the Scriptures — to resign themselves to that stultification of their species in degrading equality with inferior creatures; to that retrogression which fixed their intelligence forever at the level of the gestures made by an acrobatic automaton; to that great fear of life which would eventually bend their backs in bondage as a mark of their animal state and imprint upon them the wistful bewilderment that forms a basic trait of their tragicomic nature!

This is what had aroused my ill humor, buried deep in some atavistic limbo, on the very verge of success. Through millions of years the magic power of speech kept stirring in the simian soul; but against that temptation which was about to pierce the dark shadows of animal instinct, ancestral recollections that permeated his species with some instinctive horror were also raising an age-old barrier.

Yzur began to breathe his last without losing consciousness. It was a gentle death, with eyes closed, soft breathing, faint pulse, and complete tranquillity, interrupted only from time to time when he turned his sad, old mulatto-like face toward me with a heartbreaking expression of eternity. And the last afternoon, the afternoon of his death, there occurred the extraordinary event that made me decide to write this story.

Overcome by the warmth and the quiet of the growing dusk, I was dozing at his bedside when I suddenly felt myself seized by the wrist. I awoke, startled. The monkey, with his eyes wide open, was definitely dying now, and his expression was so human that it horrified me; but his hand, his eyes, drew me toward him with such eloquence that I bent over close to his face. And then, with his final breath, the final breath that crowned and dashed my hopes simultaneously, he pronounced — I am sure of it — he pronounced in a murmur (how can I classify the tone of a voice that had not spoken for ten thousand centuries?) these words, whose deep humanity served to bridge the gap between our species:

"Water, master. Master, my master. . . ."

Alberto Gerchunoff

1883-1950

one of Argentina's finest twentieth-century writers
of short stories, was also an essayist, novelist, literary
critic, and journalist. For many years he was a member of the editorial staff of La Nación, world-famous
Buenos Aires newspaper, and a contributor to its
excellent weekly literary supplement.

We tend to forget sometimes that the Hispanic
nations of the Western Hemisphere are more of a
racial melting pot than the United States. Taken
for granted, of course, is the large Indian population of the mountain regions, and also the Negro
element in the circum-Caribbean area: these have
been part of the picture since colonial times. But
great new groups of non-Spanish Europeans have
come to Latin America in the past two generations.
Argentina, for example, has absorbed millions of immigrants, among them substantial numbers from
Germany, Austria, Switzerland, England, Ireland,
Poland, and especially from Italy. All are today devoted to Argentina, which — apparently more than

any other American nation — has the happy faculty of convert-ing its newcomers into intensely patriotic citizens in an incredi-bly short space of time.

One very small group that came to Argentina just before the turn of the century was financed by Baron de Hirsch, who founded a colony for Jews being persecuted by the Russians. Alberto Gerchunoff was a young boy when he came over with his parents at that time. He quickly became profoundly and ardently Argentine.

In 1910, the one hundredth anniversary of his adopted coun-try's independence, he published a volume of short stories called Los gauchos judíos (The Jewish Gauchos), which deals with the assimilation of this agricultural and pastoral colony into the Argentine way of life. It is a fine example of regional litera-ture based on life in the province of Entre Ríos, which lies north of Buenos Aires between the Paraná and Uruguay Rivers. Gerchunoff has taken an old legend brought over from Europe by the colonists and has blended it with their new environment on the Argentine pampa.

THE OWL

✳ ✳ ✳

As JACOB RODE PAST the Reiner place he greeted them in Spanish. The old woman answered in Yiddish, and the girl asked him if he had seen Moses, who had set out that morning to look for the dapple gray.

"Moses?" asked the boy. "Was he riding the white horse?"

"Yes, the white one."

"Did he take the road to Las Moscas?"

"No," Pearl replied, "he took the San Miguel road."

"The San Miguel road? I haven't seen him."

The old woman's voice revealed her anxiety as she wailed, "It's getting late now, and my son went off with no breakfast — only a little *mate*. He didn't take a revolver. . . ."

"There's no need to worry, señora; you can ride all day around these parts and never meet a soul."

"May God hear you," Doña Eva continued. "They say there are outlaws over near the Ornstein farm."

The conversation ended with a reassuring word from Jacob. He spurred his horse and made it buck, so as to display his skill as a horseman in front of Pearl.

The sun was setting, and the afternoon was drowsing away in the hazy glow of the red-streaked sky. The yellow hue of the gardens and the pale green of the pastures, furrowed by the dark line of the brook, lent a sweet melancholy to the countryside as in the old Hebraic poems in which the shepherdesses come home with their sleepy flocks beneath the skies of Canaan. Darkness was enveloping the houses of the settlement, and the last rays of the sun reflected in brilliant flashes from the fence wires.

"It's late, daughter, and Moses isn't coming. . . ."

"There's nothing to be afraid of, mother; it's not the first time. Remember last year, on the eve of Passover, when he went with the wagon to the woods at San Gregorio? He came back with firewood the next day."

"Yes, I remember; but he was carrying a revolver. And besides, there's a settlement near San Gregorio."

An uneasy silence followed their conversation. The twilight hush was broken only by the chirping of the crickets and the croaking of the frogs in the ponds; vague noises came from the clumps of trees. An owl swooped over the corral, hooting mournfully, and lighted on a fence post.

"What an ugly bird that is!" said the girl.

The owl hooted again, and sat staring at the women with baleful eyes that filled their hearts with uneasiness.

"They say it's a bad omen."

"So they say, but I don't believe it. What do these country folk know?"

"Don't we Jews say that the raven is a herald of death?"

"Ah, that's something else again!"

The owl swooped down close to the ground and flew up to the eaves of the house, where it hooted again; then it came back to the post and fixed its gaze upon the women. Far up the road, already in deep darkness, a horse's hoofbeats sounded. The girl strained to see, using her hand to shade her eyes. She shook her head and told her mother, "No; it isn't a white horse."

From the nearby houses the breeze brought the echo of a song, one of those melancholy, monotonous chants that lament the loss of Jerusalem and exhort the daughters of Zion — "the magnificent, the only Zion" — to weep in the night so as to awaken the pity of the Lord with their tears. Automatically Pearl sang softly:

> *"Weep and lament, oh daughters of Zion. . . ."*

Then in a louder voice she sang the song of the Spanish Jews, which the teacher, David Ben-Azam, had taught her in school:

> *"We have lost Zion,*
> *We have lost Toledo;*
> *And there is no consolation. . . ."*

As her mother's anxiety continued, the girl tried to distract her by picking up their conversation again:

"Do you believe in dreams? A few days ago Doña Raquel told us something that frightened us so."

In reply the old woman related a fearsome tale of her own.

A cousin of hers, "pretty as a star," had been promised in marriage to a man in her village. He was a wagon driver, very poor, very honest, and very God-fearing. But the girl could not bring herself to love him because he was a hunchback. On the night of their formal betrothal the rabbi's wife — a saintly woman — saw a raven.

The fiancé sold one of his horses, and with the money bought a prayer book as a present for his betrothed. Two days before the scheduled marriage the engagement was broken, and the next year the girl married a rich man in the village.

The recollection of the incident affected Doña Eva profoundly. In the deepening dusk her face lengthened, and she lowered her voice as she related the uncanny tale to her daughter.

The girl married, and one after another her children died. And what of her first fiancé? The good man had died. The rabbi in the city was consulted by the family, and he studied the matter. He examined the sacred texts, and found a similar case among the old traditions. He advised the woman to return the beautiful prayer book to the dead man. In this way she would recover her peace of mind and find happiness again.

"Tomorrow night," he told her, "carry it under your right arm and return it to him."

The distressed woman said not a word in reply. The next night, when the moon came up, she set out with the prayer book beneath her arm. A steady rain beat upon her face, and her feet, slowed by fear, scarcely made headway over the hard-packed snow. When she reached the outskirts of the village she stopped, exhausted and heartsick, to seek shelter against a wall. She thought of her dead children and then of her first fiancé, whose appearance she could hardly recall after all those years. Slowly she leafed through the prayer book, with its archaic, illuminated capital letters which she loved to look at as she recited the prayers in chorus on holy days in the synagogue.

Suddenly her eyes grew dim, and when she had recovered herself the wagon driver was standing there before her, with his sorrowful face and twisted body. . . .

"This prayer book is yours, and I am returning it to you," she told him.

The specter, whose eye sockets were filled with earth, stretched out a bony hand and took the book. Then the woman, recalling the rabbi's advice, added:

"Peace be with you. Pray for me, and I shall pray God for your salvation."

Pearl sighed. Night closed in, calm and clear. In the distance the fireflies flitted about like tiny sparks and brought a vague fear of ghosts to the spirits of the old woman and the girl. And there on the fence of the silent corral sat the owl, glowering at them with its motionless, magnetic eyes. As if obsessed by some half-hidden thought, the girl continued:

"But if the gauchos say such things about that bird, it might be. . . ."

Doña Eva looked at the fence and then down the dark road. With a quavering voice, scarcely audible, she murmured, "It might be, daughter. . . ."

A sharp chill shook her. And Pearl, her own throat clutched by the same fear, drew nearer to the little old woman. At that moment they heard the galloping of a horse. Both leaned forward to hear it better, and tried to see through the pitch darkness. Their breath came in gasps, and for their heavy hearts the minutes dragged by with painful slowness.

The neighborhood dogs began to howl. The gallop kept sounding faster and nearer, and a moment later they saw the white horse come rushing up at a furious pace. Mother and daughter leaped up in terror, and from their throats came a long, piercing shriek. The sweating horse had stopped at the gate; it was riderless, and the saddle was covered with blood. . . .

Javier de Viana

1872-1926

was raised on the ranch where he was born, out on the limitless pampa of Uruguay. On his father's cattle raising estate his first teachers and constant companions were the gauchos, who inspired in him an abiding love for rich earth, good livestock, and fine horseflesh. He early absorbed the gauchos' virile outlook on life, including their glorification of physical prowess and their deep sense of personal honor. Young Javier was practically raised in the saddle until the age of eleven, when he was sent to Montevideo to begin school.

He later went on to study medicine, entered politics, and exiled himself to Buenos Aires after a Uruguayan revolution in 1904. In Argentina he became a journalist, a novelist, and a writer of short stories. In this last category he is Spanish America's most vigorous — sometimes brutally realistic — regional author.

The colorful old nineteenth-century gauchos were already legendary figures when Viana started to write, but he captures the spirit and the speech of their more modern (*if less romantic*) counterparts on the rolling pampas of Argentina and Uruguay. The coming of the railroads, barbed-wire fences, and successive waves of agricultural immigrants had already put an end to the primitive, nomadic existence of those cattle-driving centaurs of old. But they are still enshrined in the hearts of their countrymen: to be "muy gaucho" today means to be virile, courageous, intensely proud, and deeply honorable.

The tale translated here is a favorite of all anthologists; it comes from Viana's collection called Leña seca (Dry Firewood), published in 1913. His many volumes of short stories form part of the mainstream of gaucho literature in the River Plate region, from Hernández' epic poem Martín Fierro (1872) to the now classic novel Don Segundo Sombra (1926) by Ricardo Güiraldes. The student of Comparative Literature may read both these masterpieces in excellent English translations. Gaucho literature is the most typically American manifestation of Hispanic life and letters.

THE HORSE-BREAKER

* * *

H<small>E MIGHT HAVE BEEN</small> twenty-five or thirty years old —
perhaps a little older — but in any event he was quite
young.

His name was Sabiniano Fernández, and he had come to
the ranch as a horse-breaker a little more than a year
before. The ranch owner, who had a large head of half-
wild breeding horses, about fifty unbroken colts, hired him
because of his reputation as a skillful, courageous, and
painstaking worker.

He was a fine-looking fellow, Sabiniano — of medium
height, with broad shoulders, strong legs, and a rugged
face: big brown eyes, a strong, aquiline nose, full lips
topped by a fine black moustache, and a determined chin.
He spoke very little, never laughed, and there was a
suggestion of haughty disdain in his graceful bearing. He
was believed to be a rich man; it was known that he owned
a tract of land which he rented out, and that his string
of horses was unrivalled in the region. His riding gear was
expensive — silver and gold in profusion — and his money
belt was always bulging with bank notes.

If he continued in his rough and dangerous occupation
it was because he was fond of it, because breaking in
horses was his greatest joy (the more unruly and spirited
the colt, the better he liked it), and not because he cared
at all about the eight gold pesos he earned for each animal
he broke in.

He was not known to have any friends. The ranch hands respected him, but did not like him because of his arrogant and domineering temperament. On the infrequent occasions when he spoke, he did so in the form of peremptory commands, which all obeyed — willingly or unwillingly — since they were compelled to admit that he was always right, that everything he said made sense.

Toward women, as toward men, he showed polite disdain.·It was known that he had fleeting affairs, but there was no great love in his life. He seemed to be indifferent to the advances of more than one pretty girl, attracted by his virile good looks, his prowess, his arrogance, and his prestige as a master horse-breaker — a master of animals and of people.

Blasa, the ranch owner's daughter, did not escape his charm. She was a pretty little brunette, conceited and accustomed to turning young men's heads just to satisfy her feminine vanity. Sabiniano represented a conquest that would fill her with pride, and she considered her triumph an easy one because of the fascination of her youth, her beauty, and her father's wealth. She used her customary tactics on him: a languid look, as if absorbed in thought, a deliberate brush of hands on some pretext . . . and then, indifference, plus excessive graciousness toward the stranger visiting the ranch — for one was always there.

Time went by, however, and Sabiniano seemed not to notice Blasa's advances. In the dining room when the family was all together he was pleasant to her, and even deigned to smile from time to time; but if by chance they found themselves alone he was consistently aloof, on occasion to the point of rudeness.

One morning at the hitching rail he was softening up

a bridle while waiting for the ranch hands to drive the horses into the corral so he could break in a dapple gray Blasa had chosen for riding. The girl approached him and offered him a drink of *mate,* saying in a flattering tone: "Just so the dapple-gray won't throw you."

"Sabiniano isn't thrown by ponies!" he answered in a gruff voice.

Realizing that she had offended him, she added sweetly: "Hasn't any creature ever thrown you?" And drawing close to him, she brushed lightly against his shoulder with her arm.

The horse-breaker looked at her steadily, took a sip of *mate,* and answered in an icy tone: "Colts, sometimes; mares, never."

Her pride wounded to the quick, Blasa turned as red a *ceibo* blossom; her lips trembled, her eyes flashed, her fingers twitched, and her heart pounded violently. She tried to answer with a stinging remark, but the words stuck in her throat; she tried to leave with a gesture of displeasure but her legs could not move.

He handed her the *mate,* and she asked meekly, "Is it good?"

Absorbed again with his task of softening up the bridle, Sabiniano answered without looking at her: "Terrible. The leaves are burned."

The girl could take no more. "You brute!" she exclaimed, her eyes filled with tears. Snatching the *mate* gourd, she stalked off with rapid strides. Without answering a word, he kept on with his work.

A little later the herd of horses was in the enclosure, and the dapple gray of the owner's daughter had been lassoed and thrown. Sabiniano saddled him on the ground. Scorning the method of jerking at the reins without mounting, he untied the horse and made him get up by giving him a kick in the flank. The colt snorted and shrank back, trembling all over, his small ears twitching and his eyes reddened.

People were looking on — the owner and his wife, the five servant girls, the foreman and the ranch hands were there. Ten yards away, leaning against the barn door, Blasa was tracing designs on the ground with the tip of her foot and keeping her head deliberately down.

"Come and watch your colt get broken in," her father called over to her. She shrugged her shoulders without answering.

Addressing the horse-breaker, the foreman said: "Something tells me this rascal is going to give you a lot of work; he has a tricky look."

"Working is the way we earn money," answered the young man. And he calmly rolled and lighted a cigarette.

A ranch hand took the colt by the ear. Sabiniano ordered him to let go. Coming close, he seized the reins and with a sudden jump landed astride. The dapple gray trembled violently as he felt the weight. A fierce blow with the whip made him rear back on his hind legs, only to resume an expectant stance on all fours. The horse-breaker sank his spurs into the animal's flanks, and the colt, crazed with rage, put his head down between his forelegs and bucked. Snorting and frothing, he twisted first to one side and then to the other, making prodigious efforts to unseat the horseman, who kept punishing him continually with the whip and spurs.

The bystanders watched the strange duel in silence. Against her will, Blasa kept drawing closer, captured by the magnificence of the spectacle; and at the instant she reached the hitching rail the dapple gray, furious, in a wrench of superb desperation, rose upon its hind legs and fell over on its back.

Blasa screamed and covered her face with her hands. When she took them away a second later she saw an epic scene: the dapple gray was stretched out at full length on the ground and Sabiniano, with the halter in his hand and his foot resting roughly upon the animal's neck, was smiling and still holding the lighted cigarette between his lips. . . .

Then, with his lasso he struck the horse on the rump, making it get up, and with incredible agility mounted it again with one leap. The colt took off at a frenzied pace, bucking constantly, and in this fashion reached the open plain, only to return to the hitching rail ten minutes later, breathless, flecked with froth, and with reddened flanks.

The horse-breaker, pressing his legs backward and pulling hard on the reins, which made the horse touch its head to its chest, halted it and made it sit back on its haunches. He dismounted lithely, unsaddled it in a second, and began to pat it; the animal, subdued and submissive, made no attempt to rebel.

Paying no attention to the congratulations and expressions of admiration, Sabiniano went calmly to the barn to sip some unsweetened *mate*. Blasa, deeply stirred, retired to her room and did not appear again for the whole day. For more than a week she seemed angry and ill-tempered toward the young man, who appeared not to notice the change. Once at the table when they were praising his abilities as a fighter, she said with fierce scorn:

"After all, between a colt and a horse-breaker the bigger brute wins."

He let his usual cold smile play about his lips and answered calmly:

"That depends; there are some who tame horses, others who master them."

And then, in a warm tone that no one had known him to use, he added:

"To be able to master, one must first know how to master himself; no one can control others if he doesn't know self-control."

TWO MONTHS LATER, when the herd had been broken in, Sabiniano announced his departure. It was a Saturday, and he was to leave on Monday.

On Sunday there was a fiesta at the ranch; young men and women from the district had come over, and there had been dancing all afternoon. Blasa, more beautifully dressed than ever, more flirtatious than ever, danced, enjoyed herself, and seemed to be unusually gay; nevertheless, she directed no glance or word to the horse-breaker, who on his part maintained his characteristic unruffled indifference.

After supper the dancing began again with even greater enthusiasm. Sabiniano talked a while with the owner and then went out to the patio, rolled a cigarette and began to smoke, leaning against the posts of the hitching rail. It was a lovely summer evening, with a big moon in a sky of purest blue. Alone, the gaucho smoked and gazed out over the broad expanse of the sleeping countryside; a rustle of skirts made him turn his head.

Blasa approached him and said with unusual cordiality, "I've come to seek you out so you can dance a waltz with me."

"Please excuse me," answered Sabiniano calmly, "I'm tired, and I have to get up very early in the morning.

She made an angry gesture, but controlled herself and asked, "So you are really going tomorrow?"

He smiled and said, "Certainly; I always do what I set out to do."

Blasa could stand no more. Her eyes filled with tears. Throwing her arms about his neck, she exclaimed between sobs, "No. You can't go. You're not going, because I love you! Don't you know I love you, you wretch?"

Calmly, slowly, the young man replied without a trace of boasting:

"Yes, I knew it all along, just as you knew I loved you; but I wanted you this way, subdued, mastered, so that you would be happy and would make me happy. An unruly mare is no good at all!"

She held him tight, kissed his lips, and capitulating completely she exclaimed humbly and submissively, with a tender tone her voice had never had: "My master! My horse-breaker!"

Horacio Quiroga

1878-1937

*is one of the greatest short story writers of Spanish
America. Many critics consider him the best. Born
in Uruguay, he lived there until he was twenty-two.
After the death of a friend from the accidental dis-
charge of a pistol, Quiroga — though entirely blame-
less — spent the rest of his life in Argentina, a
good part of it in the jungle province of Misiones
in the extreme north of that country, where Argentine territory borders on Brazil and Paraguay.*

*Most of Quiroga's hard-hitting stories deal with
the two dominant themes in Spanish American literature — Man against Nature, or Man against Man,
with a hostile natural environment as the background. The tale we have translated here falls into
the latter category, dealing as it does with the hard-
ships of the forest workers in the hot, humid Argentine north. It comes from one of his finest collections,* Cuentos de amor, de locura y de muerte *(Tales
of Love, Madness and Death), published in 1917.*

In that same year Quiroga's wife died and he re-

turned to Buenos Aires, where in 1918 he published his famous
Cuentos de la selva (Jungle Tales) and in 1921 Anaconda.
Both these collections have animals and reptiles as the protagonists. They are unique in the Spanish language, and fully
worthy of being compared to Kipling's tales of the jungle. Among
other excellent collections published were El salvaje (The Savage) in 1920 and El desierto (The Badlands) in 1924.

Toward the end of his life Quiroga became deeply morbid,
and his stories took on overtones of horror, fantasy, psychological
abnormality, disease and death. In these tales he may be compared with Poe, de Maupassant and Chekov. Failing health
brought on a tragic mental depression which drove him to
suicide in 1937.

Quiroga, who merits a place among the world's great story-
tellers, was the pioneer in depicting man's struggle against the
South American jungle. The classic full-length novel on this
theme, which should be read by every student of Spanish American letters, was written in 1924 by the Colombian José Eus-
tasio Rivera — La vorágine, translated into English as The
Vortex.

THE CONTRACT WORKERS

✳ ✳ ✳

CAYETANO MAIDANA AND ESTEBAN PODELEY, laborers hired by the month, were returning to Posadas on the river steamer *Silex* with fifteen companions. Podeley was coming back after nine months of work, his contract completed and consequently with his passage paid for. Cayetano was returning under similar circumstances, but after a year and a half, the time it took him to settle his account.

Thin, unkempt, their shirts torn to tatters, shoeless like most of the men, dirty like all of them, the two laborers feasted their eyes on the capital city of the forest, the Jerusalem and Golgotha of their lives. Nine months up there! A year and a half! But they were coming back at last, and the still painful memories of that life of toil were fading now in anticipation of the joys awaiting them.

Only two out of a hundred workers reach Posadas with credit. For the week of glory that draws them downstream they count on the advance payment for another contract.

Cayé and Podeley disembarked, giddy with the anticipation of an orgy, and were surrounded by three or four girls. Very soon they were drunk and had signed a new contract. To do what kind of work? Where? They didn't know and didn't care. What they did know was that they had forty pesos in their pockets and credit to buy a good deal more.

Wallowing in unaccustomed ease and alcoholic bliss, submissive and staggering, they both followed the girls, who led them to a store (perhaps the contract company's store) with which a special arrangement had been made — at a percentage. There the girls renewed their fading wardrobes, buying dresses, combs and ribbons with the pesos brazenly taken from their companions.

Cayé bought himself enough extracts and lotions to bathe his new clothes in perfume; Podeley, showing better judgment, insisted on getting a worsted suit. They were grossly overcharged and too blear-eyed to see the account, probably, but in any event an hour later they heaved themselves into an open carriage wearing new shoes, a poncho over their shoulders, a .44 revolver in their belts, of course, and their pockets stuffed with cigarettes. Two girls accompanied them, very proud of the display of wealth by the workers, who reeked of black tobacco and perfumes as they rode through the streets that morning and afternoon.

Night came at last, and with it the dance halls, where the girls got them to drink. From their big cash advance in wages, they would throw down ten pesos for a bottle of beer, and get one peso and forty centavos in change, which they pocketed without even looking at it.

And so, after steady spending of further advances — an irresistible necessity in order to make up for their hard life of toil with seven days of life like fine gentlemen — the steamer *Silex* went back upstream. Cayé and Podeley, drunk like the other laborers, found a place on the deck right along with ten mules, trunks, bundles, dogs, women and men.

The following day, with clear heads now, Podeley and Cayé examined their account books for the first time since they had signed the contract. Cayetano had received 120 pesos in cash and 35 in credit; Podeley 137 pesos and 5 pesos, respectively. They looked at each other with an expression that was not one of surprise, for as contract workers they were already used to this; but they couldn't remember how they had spent a fifth of that amount. "My God!" murmured Podeley. "I'll never finish paying. . . ."

And from that moment on, the only thing he could think of was to escape from there. He looked at his .44; it was really the only thing of value he was carrying with him. Six feet away, on the top of a trunk, the other laborers were busy gambling everything they had in a game of cards. Cayé watched them for a while, smiling, as these workers always smile when they are together, for any reason; he went over to the trunk, took a card, and bet five cigars on it. A modest beginning, which perhaps would win him money enough to pay off the advance wages already received and let him go back on the same steamer to Posadas and spend a new advance. He lost. He lost the rest of his cigars. He lost five pesos, his poncho, even his shoes. The next day he won back his shoes, but nothing else.

Podeley won a box of perfumed soap that had changed owners innumerable times, which he bet against a machete and a half dozen stockings; he was quite satisfied.

Finally they arrived. The laborers climbed the endless red clay path to the heights. From there the *Silex* seemed tiny and lost on the dreary river. With cries and curses in Guaraní* they bade farewell to the steamer.

FOR PODELEY, A WOODSMAN, who earned as much as seven pesos a day, the life of a laborer was not hard. Accustomed to it, he began his new job the following day as soon as his area of forest had been allotted. He built his palm-leaf shelter — just a roof and one wall — and rigged up a bed

* The Indian language of Paraguay, northern Argentina and southern Brazil.

of eight horizontal logs; on the wall he hung his provisions for the week. Mechanically, he began his work pattern again: the cups of *mate* in silence when he got up, while it was still dark; the search for wood; breakfast at eight; back to work again, stripped to the waist, with his sweat attracting flies and mosquitoes; then lunch — beans and corn swimming in grease; and to finish up at night, after another struggle with the forest, the leftovers from noontime. In this way he would keep on working until Saturday afternoon. Then he would wash his clothes, and on Sunday go to the company store to buy provisions.

This was the one big diversion for the laborers, in spite of the fact that prices kept on rising. The same fatalism that caused them to accept this injustice dictated the elemental duty of getting revenge by working as little as possible. And if this aim was not present in the hearts of all of them, the laborers all felt the same sense of injustice and a deep hatred of the boss, who, in turn, watched his men night and day, especially the contract workers.

Cayetano, meanwhile, was constantly thinking about his escape. Fortunately, he had carefully kept his .44, which he needed to protect himself against the boss' Winchester rifle.

It was now the end of October, and the steady rain was undermining the workers' health. Podeley, free of sickness up until then, felt so tired one day when he reached his work area that he stopped and looked all about him without the will to do anything. He started back to his shelter, and on the way felt a slight tickling sensation in his spine. He knew very well what that tiredness and tickling meant. Resigned to it, he sat down and had some *mate*. A half hour later a deep and prolonged chill went up and down his back: it was *el chucho* — malaria. There was nothing he could do for it. He threw himself down on his bed, shivering with the cold and curled up under his poncho, while his teeth chattered continually.

The next day the attack, which he had not expected until nightfall, came at noon. Podeley went to the company store to get quinine. The malaria was so obvious in the worker's appearance that the clerk handed him a package from the shelf with only a glance at the sick man, who calmly placed the terrible, bitter dose on his tongue.

When he got back to the forest he met the boss. "You too?" the latter said, looking at him. "That makes four. The others don't make very much difference. But you owe us money . . . How is your account?"

"I've got it almost all paid off . . . but I'm not going to be able to work. . . ."

"Bah! Take good care of yourself and it doesn't mean a thing. See you tomorrow."

"Tomorrow," said Podeley. He hurried away, for in his feet he had just felt a slight tickling sensation.

The third attack began an hour later, and Podeley was left completely exhausted. He had a dull, glazed look, as if he couldn't walk more than one or two yards. The complete rest he had for three days left him only a hunched-up hulk, shivering and chattering in his bed.

Podeley, whose previous bouts of fever had had a well-defined, periodic rhythm, felt serious misgivings about these prolonged attacks. There is fever — and there is fever. If the quinine had not ended the second attack, it was useless to stay there and die. He went back to the store.

"You again!" the boss said to him. "That's not so good. Didn't you take the quinine?"

"I did. I can't stand this fever any more . . . I can't work. If you can give me the money for my passage, I'll pay you back as soon as I'm better. . . ."

The boss surveyed that human wreck, and placed little value on the bit of life still left there.

"How is your account?" he asked again.

"I still owe twenty pesos . . . I paid you something on Saturday. I'm very sick."

"You know very well that while your account isn't settled you have to stay here. Down there . . . you could die. Get well here, and then pay off your account."

Cure a persistent fever there, where he had contracted it? Of course not. But a contract worker who leaves might not come back, and the boss preferred a dead man to a distant debtor. Podeley had never failed to settle for any-thing — the only point of pride a contract worker has, so far as his boss is concerned.

"I don't care if you have never failed to settle up!" the boss continued. "Pay your account first, and then we'll talk!"

This injustice made Podeley think of revenge at once. He went to stay with Cayé, whose attitude he knew well. They both decided to run away the next Sunday.

"Last night three workers escaped," the boss shouted to Podeley when he met him that same afternoon. "That's what you'd like, isn't it? They owed me money, too, like you! But you're going to die here before I let you out of this forest! You be careful — and all the rest of you who are listening! You've been warned!"

The determination to escape, with all its dangers — which a contract worker needs all his strength to face — is capable of holding in check even more than a persistent fever. Sunday, moreover, had come, and under pretext of going to wash their clothes they were able to elude the watchful eye of the boss. Podeley and Cayetano were soon a thousand yards from the company store. While they were sure they were not being followed they did not wish to leave the trail because Podeley travelled slowly. And even so. . . .

The strange resonance of the forest brought them from afar the sound of a voice that was shouting: "Shoot to hit them in the head! Both of them!" And a little later the boss and three peons came into view, running around a bend in the trail. The hunt was on. Cayetano cocked his revolver without stopping his flight.

"Surrender!" the boss shouted to them.

"Let's take to the woods," said Podeley. "I have no strength to use my machete."

"Come back or I'll shoot!" another voice shouted at them.

"When they are nearer . . ." Cayé began. A rifle bullet sped down the trail.

"Go on in!" Cayé shouted to his companion. And taking cover behind a tree, he fired five shots from his revolver at them. A sharp scream answered, while another rifle bullet struck the tree.

"Surrender or I'll kill you. . . ."

"Go on, go on," Cayetano urged Podeley. "I'm going to . . ."

And after firing again he slipped into the forest.

Stopped momentarily by the shots, the others now plunged ahead, firing round after round from their rifles as they followed the fugitives.

A hundred yards from the trail, and parallel to it, Cayetano and Podeley were drawing away, bending close to the ground to avoid the jungle vines. The others knew where they were, but since the attacker in the forest has a hundred chances to one of receiving a bullet in the middle of his forehead, the boss contented himself with firing his Winchester and shouting threats.

The danger had passed. The fugitives were exhausted.

Podeley covered himself with his poncho, and resting against his companion's back, suffered the reaction from that terrible effort with a two-hour attack of malarial chills and fever.

They continued their flight, always paralleling the trail, and when night finally came they made camp. The sun was high the next morning when they came to the river, the first and final hope of fugitives. Cayetano cut a dozen bamboo poles, and Podeley, whose waning efforts were expended in cutting jungle vines, hardly had time to do so before he suffered another attack of *el chucho*. Cayetano then built the raft alone, and ten seconds after it was finished they climbed aboard. The raft, carried by the current, entered the Paraná River.

At that season the nights are extremely cool, and the two workers, on opposite sides with their feet in the water, spent the night shivering with the cold. The current of the Paraná, swelled by heavy rains, kept spinning the raft around and slowly loosening the knots of the jungle vines.

All the next day they ate only two corn meal cakes, their last remaining provisions; Podeley scarcely nibbled at his. The bamboo poles, battered by the current, kept sinking little by little, and by nightfall the raft was almost awash.

All during the pitch-black night, through which their desperate eyes saw nothing, the two men kept on going down the wild river between two dark walls of completely uninhabited jungle. Submerged up to their knees, they went spinning downstream on the raft and just managed to stay afloat upon the almost separated logs, which kept dipping beneath their feet. The water was up to their chests when they reached land. Where were they? They did not know. . . . It was a hayfield. But they stretched out motionless, face down, right there on the river bank.

The sun was shining brightly when they awakened. About four hundred yards to the south they could see the River Paranaí, which they decided to ford as soon as their strength came back. But it did not return rapidly, for they had eaten virtually nothing. And for twenty hours the heavy rain turned the two rivers into raging torrents. Completely impossible! Podeley suddenly sat up, leaning on his revolver to rise, and aimed at Cayé. He was burning with fever.

"Go on, get out of here!"

Cayé saw that he could expect little from that delirium, and bent over to reach his companion with a stick. But the other insisted. "Get into the water! You brought me this far; now leave me!" The livid fingers of the sick man trembled on the trigger.

Cayé obeyed. He let himself be carried along a little by the current, and slipped out of sight beyond the hayfield. Then, with a tremendous effort, he reached the shore. From there he went back to look at his companion, but Podeley was doubled up again on the ground, with his knees to his chest, beneath the steady rain.

When Cayetano approached, he raised his head; almost without opening his eyes he murmured: "Cayé . . . oh God! . . . so cold. . . ."

The heavy autumn rain fell in white sheets all night upon the dying man, until at dawn Podeley lay still forever in his watery tomb. And in the same hayfield, held prisoner seven days by the forest, the river, and the rain, the survivor ate the few roots and worms he could find. He kept losing strength little by little until he just sat there dying of cold and hunger, with his eyes fixed upon the Paraná.

The river steamer *Silex*, which passed there at dusk, picked up the contract worker, who was by then almost dead. His joy changed to terror the next day when he realized that the steamer was heading upstream.

"I beg you, for God's sake," he wept before the captain, "don't put me off at Port X! They're going to kill me! I beg you, for God's sake!"

On its return trip the *Silex* took the worker, still suffering from nightmares, back to Posadas.

TEN MINUTES AFTER LANDING he was drunk again, had signed another contract, and was staggering to the store to buy more lotions.

Arturo Uslar Pietri

1906-

is one of Spanish America's most highly regarded modern novelists, literary critics and short story writers. He comes from an old Venezuelan family that distinguished itself nobly in the days of Bolívar the Liberator. Steeped in his country's traditions and folkways, Dr. Uslar Pietri has given us unforgettable pen portraits of Venezuela in his historical novels, particularly in Las lanzas coloradas (The Red Lances) *which, since its publication in 1936, has been translated into several European languages.*

His first volume of short stories, Barrabás y otros relatos (Barrabas and other Tales) *published in 1928, was very well received throughout Spanish America. It is from this collection that the following story has been translated. Other fine volumes of short stories written by Uslar Pietri are* Red (The Net), *published in 1936, and* Treinta hombres y sus sombras (Thirty Men and their Shadows) *in 1949.*

The jungle region depicted in this story is in the northern part of the continent, but the perils of the tropical rain forest are much the same all over South America. However, the jungle is only a small part of Venezuela. To gain a broader insight into the country and the effects of natural forces on its life and letters, the student of Comparative Literature should read also the now-classic novel Doña Bárbara, which deals with the rugged existence of the semi-nomadic cattle raising people of the vast plains that lie between the Andes and the Orinoco River. Written in 1929 by Prof. Rómulo Gallegos, former president of Venezuela, it is now available in English translation.

Dr. Uslar Pietri is one of his country's most brilliant intellectuals. He has written several splendid volumes of literary criticism, and treatises on law and economics. Professor of Political Economy at the Central University in Caracas at the age of thirty-one, he became Venezuela's Minister of Education at thirty-three. More recently, Dr. Uslar Pietri has taught Spanish American Literature at Columbia University in New York City.

THE VOICE

* * *

"NEVERTHELESS, I have killed a man. . . ."

When Brother Dagoberto said that, his black beard quivering in the iridescent glow of the flickering candle-light, all I could do was to throw the playing cards down upon the table and burst out laughing.

I had arrived in the evening after going through the jungle and the swamps in that thick, choking mist. The Indian guide kept consoling me along the way: "Don't lose hope, master; one more turn and you'll be at the house. Right away, master." And that long trail, twisting like a piece of old lacework, kept plunging endlessly on through the undergrowth.

Night was falling as I dismounted at the Mission; my poor horse was footsore, and sweat was trickling down his dark, dust-covered hide. The friars were waiting for me in the hallway, which was lighted by oil lamps. One by one the Prior introduced them to me:

"Brother Ermelindo. . . ."

"At God's service, and yours."

"Brother Froilán. . . ."

And then the last one — withdrawn, quiet, lean and wiry — with a close-cropped black beard.

"Brother Dagoberto, our good angel. . . ."

Brother Dagoberto — a name as Gothic as a pointed arch — was the one who had ventured most deeply among the wild Indian tribes. When he arrived he was a robust young man, but fevers, beriberi, sleepless nights and endless wanderings had gradually emaciated him until his skin was stretched taut over his bones. Now in very poor health, he could not venture out to make converts like the other strong friars; he spent his days in the rustic chapel praying fervently before the rough-hewn statues of Christ carved from crude logs, as if his life were fading away with one of those specks of dust that danced madly in the sunbeam that filtered through the tiny little window.

He struck me just right, as the saying goes: he made a hit with me. There was something about him that attracted me naturally, and I determined to seek his friendship. That night during dinner, as the smudge pots of dried cow dung burned beneath the table to ward off the huge mosquitoes, I got to know him better, and by the time the meal was over he was my friend. To aid digestion and pass the time, we decided to play a game of cards.

The game was a pretext for conversation. We spoke of a thousand things — silly and sublime, gay and grave. I told him the reason for my journey: in search of adventure and riches, I was on my way to join an uncle of mine who was developing some gold mines in the most remote region of that jungle. He gave me advice based upon his long experience, and told me about the strange things that happen in the jungle, about its dangers and about the precautions one must take.

"In the jungle, my son, strange and unusual things happen. You can stay in it forever without knowing how, or why; you might also kill. To kill a man in the jungle is easy, sometimes unavoidable. The jungle is always different, always dangerous."

"Come, father; don't jest. This business of killing men is a question of personality. As you can see, I have not yet begun; and as for you, there's no point even in mentioning it. . . ."

The friar kept silent a long time, as if he were thinking, remembering.

"Nevertheless, I have killed a man."

It was so unexpected, so incredible, that a laugh sprang to my lips:

"You . . . a murderer . . . Ha, ha, ha!"

The echoes of laughter died away, and Brother Dagoberto sat hunched in silence like a cat. Then in very slow and measured tones he said to me, "Yes . . . I am a murderer, as you shall hear, my son.

"It was quite a while ago. This Mission was still very new, and I was still young. The Paragua Indians had risen in revolt. They destroyed the crops, closed up the mines, tore down the crucifixes, and killed our Brother Eleuterio, who was winning them over to Christianity. Men do evil things when they are angry. Then our Prior sent me to bring them back to the ways of peace and religion. As a guide they gave me the Indian José, one of the most famous pathfinders in this whole region. For him the jungle was as familiar as his old family homestead.

"We left before dawn, carrying a lantern, a pistol to defend ourselves against wild animals, and a good supply of food. We plunged into the jungle at a rapid pace. At dawn, my son, the jungle is imposing; the trees stand tall and open like green-flaming candelabra, and there is a vast and terrible silence, so profound that the slightest sound is amplified and becomes stupendous, monstrous, like a scream in the middle of an empty cathedral. The jungle is full of extraordinary things.

"The Indian kept jogging along in front of me with quick, sure steps. From time to time he would give a guttural cry to encourage himself as he went. The soft earth was studded with tracks: the cloverleaf shape of a jaguar's paw, the arrow-like shape of a deer's hoofs, the broad track left by a tapir. The sun wove a luminous spiderweb among the foliage. Now it was becoming daylight, with that pale kind of light typical of the deep forest.

"At noon the Indian said to me, 'Padre, it would be a good idea to eat now; you are tired and hungry.'

"We ate at the base of a thick tree. Then, dipping our faces into a clear spring, we gulped down water.

"We went on, and as we advanced slowly along the trail I said to him: 'Listen, José, is there much more to go?'

" 'We'll be there right away, Padre, you just wait; it's beyond that little hill over there; just a little bit more walking, and we're there.'

"That little hill was a slight rise of land, covered by trees, that stood out on the horizon. I estimated five more hours of walking, all for the love of God. . . . We trudged on and on with superhuman strength, like two beasts of burden. I was so tired that I was numb, stiff, almost paralyzed.

"I asked again, 'Is it much farther, José?'

" 'Alas, dear master, the road is strange: today it has grown much longer.'

"Now the sky was iridescent, and in half an hour at most it would be dark. Nevertheless, we kept on walking doggedly. The air was as wet as it is near a river bank, and among the trees the light was fading fast. You have no idea, my son, what a journey means in that endless jungle.

"Suddenly the Indian stopped, drew close to me, and said almost in a whisper, 'Padre, we are lost; this is not the way.'

"There was a moment of despair, of doubt. Night was falling. Then José said in his soft way, 'Don't worry, Padre; there is no danger. We'll spend the night here, and early in the morning we'll find the proper path.'

"With resignation we began to gather wood and cut

branches in order to light a fire and rig up a shelter to protect ourselves from the cold dampness and from the moon, for in the jungle the moon is harmful. In the silence the dry branches cracked loudly as they were broken off. . . .

"I heard a cry and turned, frightened; it came from the spot where José was. I ran over to him with the lantern in my hand. He was stretched out on the ground sobbing, as he clutched his leg with both hands: 'I'm going to die, master; a poisonous snake bit me.'

"I brought the light closer, and saw in his leg muscle two tiny holes that oozed two thin, steady streams of blood.

" 'I'm dying, master,' the Indian murmured.

"His voice went echoing through the jungle and came back booming, harsh and loud. In my anxiety I did what came to mind: I took the glass off the lantern and touched its soft, licking tongue of flame to the wound; his flesh burned with a sickening smell.

" 'Oh, oh, oh! Master, I am dying.'

"His skin had become brown, and showed deep cracks. I applied a compress of cool leaves, set the lantern on the ground, and sat down next to him, waiting for what might happen. From his throat came a hoarse sound like the bellowing of bulls in the slaughterhouse, and his whole body shook with a terrible chill.

"His leg had grown to monstrous size: it was like an elephant's. The inflammation was spreading rapidly. It mounted to his thigh, reached his body, and then his throat. His appearance was no longer human; he was like one of those rubber figures that are pumped full of air. He looked like a giant toad: his skin had become thick and black, like a reptile's.

"His voice was soft and pleading: 'Oh, oh, master, I am suffering so. . . .'

"His words were soft, almost — God forgive me — voluptuously feminine. He was shapeless: the inflammation had reached its height. That flesh — expanding, dilating, soft and elastic — was repugnant. At any moment it would burst like a bomb. I felt dizzy, drunk. I could see him flying into a thousand pieces, a thousand pieces that would reach the sky, a thousand pieces that would blot out the stars. . . .

"Now the voice was sweet, very sweet: 'Oh, dear master, for the love of God, kill me, dear master. I am suffering so. . . . You'll do it for me, won't you? Kill me, dear master.'

"And from the depths of the jungle the voice, changed into a scream, a shrick, an imprecation, reechoed: 'Kill me, dear master!'

"The night was filled with the scream. I felt I was going mad. What horror! It sounded hollow, muffled, like a hammer blow inside a cavern.

"His skin was becoming transparent; it could stand stretching no longer. Desperate now, I walked away a little. But the voice came howling through the trees, monstrous, terrible: 'Dear master! Oh, oh, oh!'

"What I felt was a kind of nausea, a sickness at the stomach such as must be felt by men who have drunk too much. The roaring kept closing in on me.

"The scream kept pulling me closer, just as a jaguar's eyes attract a bird. It kept pushing me toward him.

" 'Kill me, for the love of God!'

"There he was again in front of me, breathing his last, begging. The Lord knows, it wasn't I. It was something irresistibly superhuman that put the pistol into my hand. . . .

"The whole jungle roared, filled with his cry: 'You'll do it for me, won't you?'

"The screaming suddenly stopped . . . the voice was still. A mighty, howling, frightful, thundering crash came rumbling through the jungle. The voice would be heard no more. . . ."

Rubén Darío

1867-1916

was a Nicaraguan by birth, but belongs to the entire
Spanish-speaking world, on both sides of the Atlantic.
The movement of which he was the chief exponent
— Modernism — was the first to bring Latin American letters into the mainstream of world literature,
and the first American literary movement to influence the Spanish motherland.

Because Darío's poetry is so dazzling, the student
of Comparative Literature tends to forget that the
Nicaraguan author was also a prose writer of singular
merit. Indeed, his first major work Azul (Blue),
which burst like an atomic bomb whose fall-out
spread over the whole Hispanic world, contains both
prose and verse. It is from this brilliant first collection, published in Chile in 1888, that we have translated the story that follows.

At that time Darío was a newspaperman in Santiago. Later he became a foreign correspondent for
La Nación of Buenos Aires, where his second volume
of verse — Prosas profanas (Lay Hymns) — was

published in 1896. In the twentieth century he served his country in the diplomatic corps as Minister to Paris and Madrid. In the latter city his third great work — Cantos de vida y esperanza (Songs of Life and Hope) — *was published in 1905. Other fine volumes followed, but the three already cited were his most representative, and in them Modernism reached its zenith.*

Modernism was essentially a protest against the pedestrianism of poetry and the colorlessness of prose as written in the latter half of the nineteenth century. It was also an artistic reaction that sought escape from the smothering middle class materialism of stuffy Victorian society. For this reason the new movement brought with it not only metrical innovations but also a revitalized vocabulary of aristocratic refinement, exquisite beauty, and exotic cosmopolitanism. It is no coincidence that the young man in our story is a sculptor whose special love is oriental art.

The reader will notice even through the translation that Darío's poetic prose abounds in words that evoke elegance, delicacy, softness and subdued colors.

THE DEATH OF THE EMPRESS
OF CHINA

* * *

LIKE A HUMAN JEWEL, delicate and finely wrought, that dainty girl with skin of palest pink lived in the cottage whose tiny parlor had drapes of faintest blue. It was her jewel case.

Who was the owner of that delightful, joyous bird with eyes of black and mouth of red? For whom did she sing her song divine when smiling Spring's lovely face shone through the triumphant sun, opened the flowers in the fields, and stirred the fledglings in their nests? Suzette was the name of the little bird that had been placed in a cage of silk, plush and lace by a dreamy artist-huntsman who had caught her one morning in May when the air was drenched with sunlight and many roses opened wide.

A year and a half before, Recaredo — a whim of his father's: it wasn't his fault he was named Recaredo — had married. "Do you love me?" — "I love you." — "And you?" — "With all my heart."

Beautiful was the golden day, after the priest had played his part. They had gone at once to the springtime countryside to enjoy in freedom the delights of love. The bell-flowers and wild violets, fragrant there beside the brook, gossiped in their windows of green leaves when the two lovers went by, his arm around her waist, her arm about his, as their ardent lips, in youth's full bloom, set kisses free. Came then the return to the big city, to the nest filled with the perfume of youth and the glow of delight.

Have I said as yet that Recaredo was a sculptor? Well, if

I haven't, you are now informed: he was a sculptor. In the little house he had his studio, with its profusion of marbles, plaster casts, bronzes and terracottas. Passersby would hear at times through the window gratings and blinds a voice singing and a hammer ringing: Suzette and Recaredo — the throat that poured forth a song, and the metallic tap of the chisel.

Then there was the unending idyll of their wedded bliss. On tiptoe she would come to where he was working, let her hair flood over the nape of his neck, and kiss him quickly. Quietly, ever so quietly, he would steal to where she lay half asleep upon her divan, a book open upon her lap, her shoes still on her tiny feet, and her black-stockinged legs crossed one upon the other. There the kiss is full upon the lips, a kiss that takes her breath away and makes her eyes open wide, with a glow beyond description.

And amid all this, the laughter of the blackbird, a blackbird kept in a cage, that becomes sad and will not sing when Suzette plays Chopin. The blackbird's bursts of laughter were indeed something! "Do you love me?" — "Don't you know?" — "Do you love me?" — "I adore you!" By now the horrid creature would be laughing with all his might. He would be taken from his cage, flutter all around the blue-tinted little parlor, and come to rest upon the head of a plaster Apollo or on the javelin of an old Teuton done in dull bronze. Tiiiiirit . . . rrrrrtch fii . . . ! My but he was ill bred and insolent at times in his chattering! But he was pretty upon the hand of Suzette, who used to pet him, press his beak between her teeth until she drove him frantic, and sometimes say with a stern voice that trembled with tenderness: "Mr. Blackbird, you're a great big rascal!"

When the two lovers were together they would fix each other's hair. "Sing," he would say, and she would sing slowly; and though they were just two poor young people in love, they felt themselves to be handsome, proud, and regal: he looked upon her as an Elsa, and she upon him as a Lohengrin. For Love (ah, youth, full of warmth and dreams!) places a blue crystal before our eyes and grants us infinite joys.

How they loved each other! He thought her more beautiful than the stars in heaven; his love ran the whole gamut of passion, and he was now tender, now tempestuous in his loving, and at times almost mystic. Occasionally one might have said that the artist was a theosophist who saw in his beloved wife something supreme and superhuman, like Rider Haggard's Ayesha.* He inhaled her fragrance as he would a flower's, he smiled at her as he would at a star, and felt proudly masterful as he pressed to his breast that adorable head, which, when still and lost in thought, could be compared to the priestly profile on the medallion of a Byzantine empress.

Recaredo loved his art. He had a passion for form: he would hew from marble nude, graceful goddesses with white eyes, serene and sightless. His studio was peopled by a throng of silent statues, metal animals, gruesome gargoyles, griffons with long, leafy tails, and Gothic creatures inspired perhaps by occultism. And above all, his great hobby — Japanese and Chinese curios. In this, Recaredo was a connoisseur. I don't know what he would have given to be able to speak Chinese or Japanese. He knew the best albums, he had read and adored fine, exotic writers like Loti and Judith Gautier, and he made sacrifices to acquire genuine works from Yokohama, Nagasaki, Kyoto, Nanking or Peking: knives, pipes, ugly and mysterious masks like

* Exotic heroine of the novel of the same name.

the faces in hypnotic dreams, cute dwarf mandarins with gourd-shaped paunches and slanting eyes, monsters with huge, frog-like mouths wide open and full of teeth, and tiny Tartar soldiers with frowning faces.

"Oh!" Suzette would say to him, "I hate your sorcerer's den, that terrible studio, that strange sanctuary that steals you from my caresses."

He would smile, leave his worshop, his temple of rare bric-a-brac, and hasten to the little blue parlor to see and pet his charming human jewel, and to hear the crazy, happy blackbird sing and laugh.

That morning when he came in he saw his sweet Suzette stretched out sleepily near a vase of roses that rested upon a three-legged stool. Was she the Sleeping Beauty in the forest? Dozing there, her shapely body outlined beneath a white robe, her chestnut hair all tumbled in curls on one of her shoulders, and her entire being giving off a delicate, feminine fragrance, she was like a delightful figure in one of those lovely tales that begin: "Once upon a time there was a king. . . ."

He awakened her: "Suzette, my lovely one!" His face was gay, his dark eyes shone beneath the red fez he wore as a work cap, and he bore a letter in his hand. "A letter from Robert, Suzette. The rascal is in China! 'Hong Kong, January 18th. . . .'"

Suzette, slightly drowsy, had sat up and taken the paper from him. So that globe trotter had reached such a far-off place! 'Hong Kong, January 18th. . . .' It was funny. A fine chap, that Robert, with a mania for travelling. He would reach the ends of the earth. A great friend, Robert; like one of the family. He had left two years earlier for San Francisco, California. Was there ever such a madcap!

She began to read:

Hong Kong, January 18th.

Dear Recaredo:

I came and I saw. I have not conquered yet.

In San Francisco I heard about your marriage, and was delighted. I took a mighty leap and landed in China. I've come as an agent for a California firm that imports silks, lacquers, ivory and other Chinese articles. Along with this letter you should receive a present that will suit you perfectly, in view of your fondness for things from this yellow land.

My very best to Suzette. Please accept this gift as a remembrance from

Your friend,
Robert.

And that was all. They both burst out laughing. The blackbird, in his turn, shook the cage with an outburst of screeching notes.

The box had come — a fair-sized box, covered with customs stamps, numbers, and letters that made it clear that the contents were very fragile. When the box was opened the mystery came to light. It was a delicate porcelain bust — a splendid bust of a smiling woman, pale and enchanting. At the base it bore three inscriptions, one in Chinese characters, another in English, and another in French: *The Empress of China.*

The Empress of China! What Asian artist's hands had molded those mysterious, alluring lines? She wore her hair pulled back tight, and had an enigmatic face with the exotic, downcast eyes of a celestial princess, a sphinx-like smile, and a neck held high upon soft shoulders wrapped in a ripple of dragon-embroidered silk. All of these lent magic to the wax-white porcelain, flawless in its simplicity.

The Empress of China! Suzette passed her pink fingers

lightly over the graceful sovereign's slightly slanted eyes, with their curved eyelids folded beneath the fine, nobly-arched eyebrows. She was happy. And Recaredo felt pride in the possession of his porcelain. He would make her a special little nook so she could live and reign in solitary splendor, like the Venus de Milo in the Louvre, sheltered imperially beneath the covering vault of her sacred abode.

This he did. At one end of the studio he partitioned off a small area, using silk screens decorated with designs of rice fields and cranes. The yellow note predominated, in its entire range — gold, flame, ochre, autumn glow — until it became a pale yellow fading into an off-white. In the center, upon a black and gold pedestal, the exotic empress stood smiling. Around her, Recaredo had placed all his Japanese and Chinese curios, and above her a large Nipponese parasol painted with camelias and broad, blood-red roses.

It was laughable when the artist-dreamer, putting aside his pipe and chisel, would come before the empress to make salaams with his hands crossed upon his chest. Once, twice, ten and twenty times he would visit her: it was an obsession. Every day he used to place fresh flowers for her in a lacquer bowl from Yokohama. At times he went into transports of rapture before the Asian bust, whose motionless majesty moved him to delight. He studied every slightest detail: the curve of her ears, the bow of her lips, the polish of her nose, the fold of her eyelids. The famous empress was his idol!

Suzette would call him from afar: "Recaredo!"

"I'm coming!" And he would keep on gazing at his work of art until Suzette came to drag him away with kisses.

One day the flowers disappeared from the lacquer bowl as if by magic.

"Who took the flowers?" called the artist from his studio. "I did," answered a vibrant voice through the half-opened curtain. It was Suzette, all flushed, her dark eyes flashing.

Down in the innermost recesses of his brain, Recaredo the artist-sculptor would say to himself: "What can be the matter with my little wife?" She ate practically nothing. Those fine books, whose pages had been cut by her ivory paper-knife, remained in the little black bookcase un-opened and lonesome for the soft, pink hands and the warm, fragrant lap. Recaredo could see that she was sad. What can be the matter with my little wife? At table she would not eat. She was despondent — so despondent! The husband used to glance at her sometimes out of the corner of his eye, and he saw that hers were listless and moist, as if she were about to cry. And when she answered she would speak like a child who has been refused a piece of candy. What can be the matter with my little wife? Nothing! She would say that "Nothing" with a plaintive voice, and there were tears between the two syllables.

Oh, Recaredo! The trouble with your little wife is that you are a dreadful man. Haven't you noticed that since that precious Chinese empress came into your home the little blue parlor has grown sad, and the blackbird doesn't sing or pour out his pearly peals of laughter? Suzette plays Chopin, and slowly brings forth the morbid, moody melody from the tinkling, black piano. She is jealous, Recaredo! Her illness is jealousy, stifling and searing like a fiery serpent coiled about her heart. Jealousy!

Perhaps he understood, for one afternoon he spoke these words to the girl of his heart, face to face, over a steaming cup of coffee: "You are too unjust. Can you possibly think I don't love you with all my being? Can't you read in my eyes what there is in my heart?"

Suzette burst into tears. He loved her? No, he did not love her any longer! Those lovely, shining hours had fled, and those echoing kisses were gone, too, like birds in flight. He no longer loved her. And he had abandoned her — Suzette, who saw in him her faith, her delight, her dreams, her king — for that other woman.

Another woman? Recaredo jumped up. She was mistaken. Could she be saying that because of that blonde Eulogia, to whom he had once written madrigals? She shook her head: "No."

Was it because of that rich woman Gabriela, with her long black hair and skin white as alabaster, whose bust he had done? Or that dancer, Luisa, with her wasp-like waist and incendiary eyes? Or the chic little widow Andrea, who put her red, feline tongue out between her gleaming, ivory-white teeth when she laughed? No, it was none of those. Recaredo was completely amazed.

"Look, dear little girl, tell me the truth. Who is she? You know how much I adore you, my Elsa, my Juliette, my life, my love. . . ."

So much true love throbbed in those halting, trembling words that Suzette, her eyes reddened but dry by now, stood up with her lovely, aristocratic head held high:

"Do you love me?"

"You know full well I do!"

"Then let me take revenge upon my rival. She, or I; choose. If it is true that you adore me, will you let me remove her from your path forever, so that I alone remain, confident of your love?"

"Go right ahead," said Recaredo. And as he watched

his stubborn, jealous little bird depart, he continued sipping his ink-black coffee.

He had not taken three sips when he heard a great crash inside his studio. He went there. What did his eyes behold? The bust had disappeared from the black and gold pedestal, and on the floor, among tiny, toppled mandarins and fallen fans, were pieces of porcelain being ground beneath Suzette's small shoes. All flushed, and with her hair down, awaiting his kisses, she said to her astonished husband amid peals of silvery laughter:

"I am avenged! Now the Empress of China is dead for you forever!"

And as the ardent reconciliation of their lips began in the tiny blue parlor, now filled with joy, the blackbird was convulsed with laughter in his cage.

Amado Nervo

1870-1919

Mexico's most famous Modernist, studied for the priesthood but never took his final vows; he left the seminary to carve a career in journalism, editing, and creative writing. He was also a contributor to the Modernist Revista azul *(Blue Review) in Mexico City until the untimely death of its young editor, the poet Manuel Gutiérrez Nájera, who had taken the pen name* El Duque Job — *indicative of aristocracy and suffering — so characteristic of Modernist aesthetics. Nervo then led the movement in Mexico by founding the* Revista moderna, *which continued until 1903.*

From 1905 to 1918 he served in the Mexican legation in Madrid, where he wrote many of his best poems and collections of short stories. He died in Montevideo in 1919, while he was the Mexican Minister to Uruguay. No doubt the reader has noted in these biographical sketches that the Hispanic nations appoint men of letters to serve in their diplomatic corps — evidence of the great prestige at-

tached to literature in Latin America. This international exchange of eminent writers has helped to diffuse literary influences throughout the Spanish-speaking world.

Nervo's works are characterized by an inner serenity of spirit tinged with an almost mystic melancholy. In his later years there is a pantheistic, even oriental tone to his work, for he had become deeply interested in the principles of Buddhism. His submissive acceptance of destiny is clear in the titles of some of his final volumes of verse and prose: Serenidad (1914), Elevación(1916) *and* Plenitud (1918).

Nervo was frequently preoccupied with the subject of death. The ironic story translated here deals with the civil warfare in Mexico at the time of Maximilian and Carlotta in the 1860's. It comes from his collection Almas que pasan (Fleeting Souls), *published while he was in Madrid in 1906. Little did Nervo know that four years later his country was to be plunged into the greatest revolution and series of civil wars in its long and tragic history.*

ONE HOPE

*　*　*

IN ONE CORNER of a room that had been fixed up as a
chapel the young soldier Luis, overwhelmed by the
sheer weight of his misfortunes, was thinking. He was
thinking of the bygone days of his childhood, filled with
happiness and affection showered upon him in the roomy,
peaceful home that belonged to his family. It was one of
those big, provincial houses — massive and rambling —
with spacious halls, a garden, an orchard, and stables. Its
wide windows, which opened upon the single street of a
medium-sized city not far, indeed, from the one in which
he was about to die, were barred by strong, curved gratings
that displayed with conservative, manly grace their
wrought-iron rosettes.

He recalled his adolescent years, his first dreams —
nebulous as starlight — and his love (crystal-pure, mysterious, shy as a mountain fawn, and more secret than
declared) for the little blonde girl still in petticoats, who
was hardly old enough to spell out the meaning of books
and of life. . . .

Then there unfolded before his eyes the clear canvas of
his impetuous youth, his gay companions, and his relationship — now serious — with the blonde girl of earlier days,
who had grown to womanhood and was now praying for
his safe return — alas! — in vain. . . .

And finally he came to the most recent period in his life,
to the moment of patriotic fervor that made him join the
Liberal party, which was threatened with extinction by the

reactionaries, who this time were being aided by a foreign power. Then he saw again the moment when, after several skirmishes, an unlucky turn of war's fortunes had brought him to this frightful predicament. Caught with weapons in his hands, made prisoner, and offered — along with several comrades — in exchange for the lives of some reactionary officers, he had seen his last hope vanish because the proposal for exchange arrived late, after the Liberals — his colleagues — had already shot the Conservative prisoners.

He was going to die, then. This idea, which had left his conscious thinking for a moment — thanks to the pleasant excursion through the happy recollections of his childhood and youth — suddenly returned in all its horror, making him shudder from head to foot.

He was going to die . . . *to die!* He could not believe it, and yet the truth was too terribly evident. It was enough just to look about him: that improvised altar, that old image of Christ with outstretched arms upon whose emaciated body the yellowish candlelight fell flickering mysteriously, and the prison guards right there in full view through the grating in the door. He was going to die, just as he was — strong, young, wealthy, and loved. And all for what? For some abstraction called Country and Party. And what was his country? Something very indefinite, very vague for him in those moments of confusion; while life — the life he was going to lose — was something real, very real, concrete and definite . . . it was *his* life!

"My country! To die for my country!" he thought. "But in its detached and serene unawareness my country will not even know that I have died for it. . . ."

"And what difference does it make, so long as you know it?" replied some mysterious subconscious, deep within him. "Your country will know it through your own knowledge and your own thought, which is a portion of its thought and its collective conscience. That is enough. . . ."

No, that was not enough; and above all, he did not want to die: his life was very much his own, and he was not resigned to their taking it away from him. A mighty impulse toward self-preservation rose in revolt within him and surged uncontrollably through his whole being, torturing him and filling him with violent dissent.

At times the cumulative fatigue from earlier sleeplessness, the intensity of his pent-up thoughts, and the very enormity of his grief all overwhelmed him, and he dozed a little. But then his abrupt awakening and the immediate, clear and sudden realization of his doom — forgotten for a moment — were an unspeakable torment, and the unfortunate wretch, placing his hands over his face, would sob so audibly that his guards would peer through the grating, their bronze faces revealing the age-old indifference of the Indian.

2

A SHORT, WHISPERED CONVERSATION was heard at the door, and at once it was opened softly to let in a sombre figure whose garb almost blended into the blackness of the night, which was now dispelling the last rays of twilight. It was a priest.

No sooner did the young soldier see him when he rose and extended his arms as if to stop him, exclaiming, "It's no use, padre; I don't want to confess!" And without waiting for that shadow to reply, he continued with mounting irritability, "No; I will not confess. It is useless for you to come and take the trouble. Do you know what I want? I want my life. I want them to spare my life; it's mine, very much mine, and they have no right to take it from me! If they are Christians, why are they killing me? Instead of sending you to me to open the doors of eternal life, let them begin by not closing the doors of this one. . . . I don't want to die! Do you understand? I rebel against dying! I am young, healthy, and rich; I have a mother and father, and a sweetheart who adores me; life is beautiful, very beautiful for me. . . . To die on the field of battle, in the clash of combat beside your fighting comrades when your blood is stirred by the trumpet's blare. . . . good, good! But to die obscurely and pathetically, with your back against some musty garden wall in the corner of a dirty little plaza at the break of dawn, without anyone's even knowing that you died like a man . . . padre, padre, that is horrible!" And the unhappy wretch threw himself upon the floor, sobbing.

"My son," said the priest, when he felt that he could be heard, "I do not come to bring you the consolation of religion; on this occasion I am the emissary of men and not of God. If you had listened to me calmly from the beginning you would have avoided the paroxysm of grief that is making you sob that way. I come precisely to bring you your life . . . do you understand? . . . that life you were begging for with such inordinate anguish a moment ago, the life that is so precious to you! Listen to me carefully, and try to overcome your nerves and your emotions, for we have no time to lose. I have come in here on the pretext of hearing your confession, and everyone must think that you are confessing; kneel, then, and listen to me.

"You have powerful friends who are interested in your fate, and your family has done the impossible in order to save you. Since they couldn't obtain your pardon from the Commandant, they have succeeded — with unusual difficulties and untold risks — in bribing the leader of the platoon assigned to shoot you. The rifles will be loaded with only gunpowder and wadding; when you hear the volley you will fall like the others taken with you to the place of execution, and you will lie still. The darkness of the hour will help you to act out this little drama. Pious hands of the Brothers of Mercy, who have already agreed to help, will pick you up from the spot as soon as the platoon moves off, and will hide you until nightfall, when your friends will aid your escape. The Liberal troops are advancing upon the city, which they will undoubtedly besiege within a few hours; you can join them if you wish. So . . . you know everything; now say aloud the prayer 'I, miserable sinner . . .' while I pronounce the words of absolution. Try to control your joy during the time that remains before the execution so that no one will suspect the truth."

"Padre," murmured the officer, so overwhelmed with happiness that he could scarcely speak, "may God bless you!"

And then, suddenly seized by a horrible doubt, he added, trembling:

"But is all this the truth? This isn't just a pious deception to ease my final hours . . . ? Oh, that would be wicked, padre."

"My son, a trick of that kind would be the greatest of misdeeds, and I am incapable of committing it. . . ."

"Of course, padre; forgive me. I don't know what I'm saying. I am out of my mind with joy!"

"Be calm, my son, very calm. Until tomorrow, then; I shall be with you at the solemn moment."

3

THE DAY WAS HARDLY BREAKING — a grey, raw, February dawn — when the prisoners to be shot, five in all, were taken from the jail. Accompanied by the priest, who prayed with them, they were led to a dismal little rock-strewn plaza, enclosed by half-fallen walls, where executions were usually carried out. Our Luis marched along among them with firm step and head held high, but his heart was filled with a strange emotion and a deep desire for a quick conclusion to that horrible farce.

When they reached the plaza the five prisoners were placed in a row a short distance from one another, and at a command the accompanying platoon divided into five groups of seven men each, in accordance with an assignment made earlier in the barracks. The colonel of the regiment, who was witnessing the execution, instructed the priest to bandage the prisoners' eyes and then to withdraw a short distance. The padre did so, and the platoon leader issued the preparatory commands in a curt, clipped voice.

The faint red of daybreak was beginning to tint the tiny clouds in the east with a pale, melancholy glow, and the silence of the early dawn was broken by the clang of a churchbell nearby, ringing the first call to Mass. Suddenly a sword flashed in the air, a deafening volley echoed brokenly across the plaza, and the five men fell tragically in the pink half-light of early day.

The platoon leader immediately had his men parade past the executed prisoners and salute them with an "Eyes right!" Then with a few words of command he made ready to return to the barracks, while the Brothers of Mercy prepared to pick up the bodies.

At that moment a ragamuffin — one of the large group of early risers who were watching the execution — pointed to Luis, who was lying stretched out at full length, and shouted in a high-pitched voice, "That one is alive! He moved a leg. . . ."

The platoon leader halted, hesitated a moment, and tried

to say something to the urchin; but his eye met the cold, questioning, commanding glance of the colonel. Taking his huge Colt .45 from the holster he was wearing, he stepped toward Luis — who was so horror stricken he could scarcely breathe — placed the muzzle to his left temple, and fired.

Gregorio López y Fuentes

1895 -

was born and brought up on a ranch in rural Mexico. He taught Indians in an elementary school in his native state of Veracruz, and later was called to become a Professor of Education at the Teachers College in the Federal District (Mexico City). Although he subsequently gave up academic life for a literary career, his work as a newspaper editor, novelist and short story writer reveals his continuing interest in the field of rural education.

López y Fuentes is one of the great novelists of the Mexican Revolution which began in 1910. His masterwork is El indio (The Indian), *for which he received the national prize in literature when it was published in 1935. Along with Mariano Azuela's* Los de abajo (The Underdogs) *and Martín Luis Guzmán's* El águila y la serpiente (The Eagle and the Serpent), *this novel gives us a stark picture of the tragic fate of the Mexican peons and Indians during the turbulent times of Porfirio Díaz, Carranza and Pancho Villa. All three of these powerful*

novels have been translated into English; for an understanding
of modern Mexico, the student of Comparative Literature should
surely read them. In many cases the Indians were exploited by
the local military chiefs in the name of the Revolution: they
were conscripted and died without even knowing what they were
fighting for in the futile conflicts and personal political rivalries
among the leaders.

The story translated here dates from more recent times, after
the country had settled down again, and had begun to con-
solidate the hard-won gains of the Revolution. In 1943 López y
Fuentes wrote a collection called Cuentos campesinos de Méx-
ico (Mexican Country Tales) for use as a text in the rural
schools. It is from this collection that our simple but revealing
story is taken.

A LETTER TO GOD

* * *

THE HOUSE — the only one in the whole valley — stood at the top of a low hill that looked like one of those primitive, truncated pyramids some wandering tribes abandoned when they moved on. From there you could see the meadows, the river, the stubble pasture, and next to the corral the field of ripe corn with beans blossoming purple among the stalks — the unmistakable sign of a good crop. The only thing the earth needed was a good rain, or at least one of those heavy showers that form puddles between the rows. To doubt that it would rain would have been the same as mistrusting the experience of veteran farmers who believed in planting on a certain day of the year.

Lencho, who knew the country well, had spent the morning scanning the sky to the northeast.

"Now at last the rain is really coming, old girl."

And his wife, who was cooking dinner, replied: "May God grant it."

The older children worked in the field while the younger ones played near the house until their mother called to them all: "Come for dinner . . . !"

It was during the meal that great drops of rain began to fall, as Lencho had predicted. Mountainous masses of clouds could be seen coming from the northeast, and the air was fresh and cool. The man went out to fetch some implements that had been left on a stone fence, just to feel the pleasurable sensation of the rain on his body. When he came in he exclaimed:

"These are not drops of water falling from the sky, they are bright coins: the big drops are ten-centavo coins, and the little drops are the fives. . . ."

And he gazed with contented eyes at the field of ripe corn and beans in blossom, all veiled in the filmy curtain of rain. But suddenly a strong wind began to blow, and hailstones as big as acorns started to come down with the raindrops. These indeed looked like new silver coins. The children dashed out into the rain to pick up the largest of the icy pearls.

"This is really very bad," the man exclaimed with chagrin. "Let's hope it stops soon."

But it did not stop soon. For an hour the hail came down upon the house, the garden, the mountain, the corn, and the whole valley. The field was white, as if covered with salt; the trees were left leafless, the corn destroyed, the beans left without a blossom. And Lencho's heart was filled with grief.

After the storm had passed Lencho told his children as he stood in the middle of the field: "A cloud of locusts would have left more than this; the hailstorm left nothing. This year we'll have no corn or beans. . . ."

The night was one of weeping.

"All our work for nothing!"

"And no one to help us!"

"This year we shall be hungry!"

But in the hearts of all who lived in that solitary house in the middle of the valley there was one hope — the help of God.

"Don't be so upset, even though it's a hard blow. Remember that being hungry never kills anybody!"

"That's what they say — being hungry never kills anybody."

And during the night Lencho thought a great deal about

what he had seen in the village church on Sundays: a triangle, and inside the triangle an eye. An eye that seemed very big, an eye — as they had explained it to him — which sees everything, even what is in the depths of one's conscience.

Lencho was an uncouth peasant who worked hard in the fields, but he knew how to write. At daybreak the following Sunday, having strengthened himself in the conviction that there is Someone who watches over us, he began to write a letter that he would carry personally into town and drop in the mail. It was nothing less than a letter to God!

"Dear God," he wrote, "if You do not help me, I and my whole family will be hungry this year. I need a hundred pesos to sow again, and to live on while the new crop is growing, because the hailstorm . . ."

He wrote "To God" on the envelope, put the letter inside, and went into town, still worried. At the post office he put a stamp on the letter and dropped it into the mailbox.

An employee who was a mailman and also an assistant at the post office came over to his boss and, laughing heartily, showed him the letter addressed to God. Never in all his days as a mailman had he come upon that house. The postmaster, fat and jolly, began to laugh, too, but suddenly became serious; and as he tapped the table with the letter he observed, "What faith! Oh, that I had the faith of the man who wrote this letter! To believe as he believes; to wait with the confidence he feels as he waits; to start corresponding with God!"

And in order not to disillusion that abundant faith, revealed by a letter that could not be delivered, the postmaster had an idea: to answer the letter. But when he opened it he found that in order to do so, something more would be needed than good will, paper and ink. He kept on with his plan, however. He asked his helper for some money, he himself gave part of his salary, and several friends of his were induced to give something "for a charitable cause."

It was impossible for him to accumulate the hundred pesos requested by Lencho, and he could send the peasant only a little over half. He put the bills into an envelope addressed to Lencho, and with them a letter that had only one word, as a signature: God.

The following Sunday Lencho came in, a little earlier than usual, to ask if there was a letter for him. It was the mailman himself who handed him the letter while the postmaster, with the happy glow of a man who has done a good deed, watched through the door from his office. Lencho showed not the slightest surprise when he saw the bills — so very sure was he — but became angry when he counted the money. God could not have made a mistake, or have denied what Lencho had requested!

He went at once to the window and asked for paper and ink. At the public desk he began to write, wrinkling his brow because of the effort it cost him to express his thoughts. When he had finished he went up and bought a stamp, licked it with his tongue, and then stuck it on with a bang of his fist.

As soon as the letter fell into the drop, the postmaster got it and opened it up. It said:

"Dear God: You know that money I asked you for? Only sixty pesos reached me. Please send me the rest; I need it badly. But don't send it through the post office, because the employees are very dishonest. Lencho."

Rafael Bernal

1915 -

cultivates two types of literature not usually associated with Spanish America — the detective story
and science fiction. Interest in these fields is growing, particularly in Argentina and in Mexico. Bernal,
one of the most successful writers of this type of
story, was born in Mexico City and received his education there and in Canada. Reading in British and
North American authors no doubt influenced him
in the direction taken by his developing skill as a
writer.

In addition to poetry and drama, he has published
short stories, novels, and a study of piracy on the
high seas — Gente de mar (1905). One of his most
fantastic science fiction works is Su nombre era
muerte (Their Name Was Death), published in
1947. It deals with the thwarting of the enslavement
of mankind by insects who infect them with an unknown virus.

Of his collection of three detective tales (Tres
novelas policíacas) published in Mexico City in 1946,

two are really novelettes and the third, De muerte natural (Natural Causes), *is an expanded short story. It is this one that we have chosen for inclusion here. The reader will note how the mild-mannered anthropologist solves the murder by combining a knowledge of biology with the science of deduction made famous by Sherlock Holmes.*

This type of story has not until recently come to the fore in Latin America, but is growing in popularity among contemporary readers. In predominantly agricultural communities, crimes of passion and revenge are more prevalent; but now in the big cities of Latin America international intrigue and other types of crime have become a growing concern of their modernized police forces. Rafael Bernal has contributed much to the growth of "international" detective fiction set against a modern background, especially in the cosmopolitan capitals with their diversified reading public.

NATURAL CAUSES

*   *   *

I F THAT NEW HYPODERMIC NEEDLE, dropped from a window of the hospital, had not fallen into his hands, Don Teódulo Batanes would never have been aware of anything, and a criminal would have gone unpunished. But we must bear in mind that in order for justice to exact its stern retribution the needle had to fall precisely into the hands of Don Teódulo and not those of some other person who would have noted nothing unusual in the series of insignificant facts which led Don Teódulo to deduce what had happened that morning in the hospital. At least this is the opinion of the narrator as he meditates upon the strange means God always employs to punish and reward.

To put it more exactly, Don Teódulo had already been discharged, his thigh completely healed after the break caused when a stone head fell upon it in the museum. At noon, when he came upon the needle, he ought to have been gone, but he was a courteous man and he wanted to say goodbye to Mother Fermina, who had taken very good care of him during his illness.

He wanted, moreover, to give her a rosary with silver beads as a remembrance, and ask her to pray for him so that idols would not fall on him again and so that he would not lose his position in the Museum of Mexico again — a position he had already lost three times because he became involved in investigating things like robberies and murders that nobody asked him to investigate, such as the theft of the golden mask and the murder of the specialist in Mayan ceramics.

He was walking in the garden looking for Mother Fermina when a hypodermic needle fell in front of him from one of the windows of the surgical pavilion. Don Teódulo, who saw it falling and flashing in the sunlight, picked it up and looked at it carefully. He saw that it had a little blood on it, as if someone had used it to give an intravenous injection; by sniffing it he tried to discover what substance had been used, but the needle had no odor.

"Some careless or absent-minded doctor or intern must have dropped this needle," he thought; and looking up toward the windows he vainly tried to ascertain which window the needle could have fallen from. Observing that all of them were slightly open and that there was nobody at any of them, he continued his walk in search of Mother Fermina, intending to hand her the needle also. He was thinking about many other things, too, particularly about the reason someone might have had for tossing out the window a new and perfectly good needle.

He went all around the garden without seeing Mother Fermina, and went back into the building. In the lobby one of the sisters was scolding an intern.

"It seems unbelievable, Pedro, that you can be so careless. Losing your gown and mask! Dr. Robles was furious because you didn't arrive on time!"

"I left them in the corridor, sister," answered Pedro, "and when I got back they weren't there any longer."

"Well, I found your gown here in the lobby," continued the sister, "on that chair. Here, take it."

"Thank you, sister," answered Pedro. "But the mask is missing. . . ."

"You must have dropped it somewhere in there!"

Don Teódulo heard the conversation, bowed to the sister, and continued toward his room to get his suitcases. He was sorry to leave the hospital. How well he was treated there, with all those nice nuns to carry out his slightest wish, those tasty meals so spotlessly served, and that complete quiet for reading and studying! What a contrast with his boarding house, and with the housekeeper who was always insinuating that Don Teódulo was absent-minded and impractical, and that she was letting him stay on as a matter of charity — when he paid his board religiously every month!

Thinking of these things, Don Teódulo did not go directly to his room but to the refectory, expecting to find Mother Fermina there and to console himself a little by talking to her, for she had always shown so much liking for him.

In one of the corridors he met a nurse.

"Good afternoon, Sister Lupe," he said.

"Good afternoon, Don Teódulo," answered the nurse. "So you're leaving?"

"Unfortunately, that is the truth or fact," he said, with his queer custom of speaking in synonyms. "Now that my leg is all better or cured, I am going back to my job or work; but as long as I live I shall have pleasant memories of you all, and I shall come to call upon or visit you frequently."

There was no one in the dining room: it was still early, and the room was empty. Farther on, he came to the visitors' room, which was nearly full. On one side of it sat the relatives of Doña Leocadia Gómez y González de la Barquera, millionaire widow whose appendix had been removed that morning. All of them were stiff, bored, and serious, as they had been on all the preceding days they had come to visit the sick woman. Don Teódulo already knew them by sight: the patient's brother, Don Casimiro, with his big, black, dyed mustache, his correct attire, and two or three strands of hair trying to cover his bald spot; Doña María, her sister, tall and withered, dressed in black; the two nephews, Juan and Ambrosio, well dressed and well groomed, with worn and dissipated faces; and the niece, Clara, stylish and sophisticated, pretty and painted, the only one that seemed capable of smiling. He knew very well that all of them were there only because Doña Leocadia, the woman who had been operated upon, was the rich member of the family. The patient had been removed from the operating theater and taken to her room more than an hour before; they were only waiting for her to wake up so they could go in to see her.

Don Teódulo glanced around the room in a vain search for Mother Fermina, and was just leaving when he saw her come in hurriedly and go over to Don Casimiro. She said something to him in a low voice, and he showed signs of amazement; he spoke to his relatives, spoke with her again, and then they all went out together down one of the corridors. Don Teódulo followed them, still hoping to talk to Mother Fermina. In the corridor outside the patient's room they met the priest. Don Teódulo conjectured that Doña Leocadia was in a critical condition, probably dying, and that she wanted to make her confession and see her relatives for the last time. Dr. Robles was coming out of the room.

"She is dead," he said. "A blood clot in her heart, which was never very strong."

The relatives bowed their heads and went into the room with the priest and Mother Fermina, closing the door behind them. The doctor commented to Sister Lupe, who was on duty in that corridor, "I can't understand it, sister;

when we brought her out after the operation she was perfectly all right."

"I went in a few minutes ago to see how she was, and found her dead," replied the sister.

"She has been dead for at least an hour," declared the doctor as he went away.

"God rest her soul," said the sister in reply; and she began the prayer for the dead.

Don Teódulo was bold enough to interrupt her: "Do you say or affirm, sister, that when you went in she was already dead? How did you know?"

"We know death, Don Teódulo," she replied.

"Were you on duty here?" asked Don Teódulo.

"Yes, and particularly watchful of this room. She is the only critical case we have . . ."

"We had, sister, we had; she is dead now. And tell me, sister: no one entered or went into the room after the operation?"

"Yes, an intern; but I couldn't recognize him. I was at the end of the corridor, and my eyesight is not too good any more."

"Thank you, sister. And now I leave you to your prayers."

Don Teódulo walked on down the corridor thinking, deliberating; something was troubling him deeply. He took out the needle and examined it carefully as he went to the hospital laboratory, where the doctor was his friend. A half hour later he came out, shaking his head. On the needle there wasn't a trace of anything — just blood. The doctor assured him that it had been used to pierce a vein, but nothing had been injected; that it was not the kind of needle the hospital ordinarily used; and that it had never been used before.

In the lobby Don Teódulo met Pedro, the absent-minded intern who had lost his gown and mask.

"They tell or inform me," Don Teódulo said to him in a jocular tone, "that you were the last one to go into Doña Leocadia's' room or sleeping quarters. Could you possibly have given her some substance or medication that caused or brought on her death?"

Young Pedro laughed heartily. He was very fond of Don Teódulo — of the way he talked, the nearsighted way he peered through his thick glasses, his timid manner — and always joked with him.

"Unfortunately," he replied, "I had no opportunity to poison her with arsenic, since I have not entered her room all morning."

Don Teódulo continued his stroll through the hospital. In another area he met a second intern, to whom he put the same question and from whom he received the same answer. Don Teódulo went along this way, asking all the interns the same thing. None of them had gone into the patient's room after she had been left there following the operation. The doctors all replied similarly when they were questioned discreetly. Don Teódulo was growing more worried all the time. At the door to the room he met Sister Lupe with a sheet.

"I am going to shroud her," she said; "they are going to take her away in a moment."

"If I were to ask you to do me a kindness or favor, sister, would you comply or assent?"

"Just ask, Don Teódulo, and please don't be so mysterious about it."

"Well, I should like you to see or observe whether the deceased or dead lady has on her arm any mark or indication of an intravenous injection."

"Why should she have it? She wasn't given any."

"Look or observe anyway," pleaded Don Teódulo with his shy, irresistible smile.

The sister entered the room and Don Teódulo stood waiting outside until she emerged a few minutes later.

"Yes," said the sister, "on her left arm she has a mark from an intravenous injection — so poorly given, in fact, that there are bloodstains in the bed. These interns are so careless at times!"

"But hadn't you told or informed me that she had been given no injection?"

"So I believed. Probably Dr. Robles prescribed something at the last moment, and it must have been administered by the intern I saw going in."

Don Teódulo sought out Dr. Robles, who had not ordered any intravenous injection at all. Pedro, questioned again, replied that he couldn't find his mask anywhere; probably one of the attendants had found it discarded around there, and had put it into the laundry. But among that day's soiled linen, which Don Teódulo carefully examined, there was no mask. When he came back to the corridor Mother Fermina was coming out of the room, and Don Teódulo called her aside.

"Mother Fermina," he said to her, "I was only looking for you or wanting to see you in order to have the pleasure — or, better said, the sorrow — of saying goodbye to you, and to give you my warmest thanks or gratitude . . ."

"Thank you, Don Teódulo," interrupted Mother Fermina. "Please wait for me in the parlor . . ."

"But right now it is necessary or urgent that I impart to you a fact or matter that cannot wait without great harm or damage."

Mother Fermina was walking along the corridors rapidly, and Don Teódulo, with his little steps, could hardly keep up with her.

"Yes," he told her, "what I shall have to do causes me great regret or grief, but I believe or think it is necessary to call the police . . ."

Mother Fermina stopped short. "What are you saying? Why should we want the police here? Has something of yours been stolen?"

"It isn't that; it has to do with something much more serious or grave. It is a question of murder. Permit or allow me to explain it to you in private."

The two of them went into the small room that housed the telephone switchboard, and there Mother Fermina listened to what Don Teódulo had to tell her. When he had finished speaking, she gave him permission to call the police.

"I'll see if I can keep those people occupied for a while," she said. "But if it is all a mistake, Don Teódulo, it will be a very costly one for us."

"There is no mistake," said Don Teódulo. "It would be best to gather the family in the dining room, which is empty, and there await or expect the police."

Mother Fermina, using a pretext, had the five relatives move into the dining room and wait there. When all were seated around a table she said to them: "There is going to be a slight delay while the doctor fills out the certificate. I beg your forgiveness."

"But he already filled out the certificate," Don Casimiro interrupted.

"Yes," continued Mother Fermina, who was clearly not practiced in the art of lying, "but it still needs the seal of the hospital; the official in charge is not here at the moment, but he will arrive shortly . . ."

"Well," said María, the dead woman's sister, "it seems to me that your hospital is run in a very lax fashion. I shall report it to the board of trustees; this sort of thing cannot be tolerated: My poor dead sister Leocadia, God rest her soul . . ."

"Amen," said Don Teódulo from a nearby table at which he was eating.

"Thank you, sir," said María, trying to smile. "Yes, indeed, Mother Fermina, as I was saying, my sister Leocadia gave vast sums to improve this hospital she loved so much, and it seems incredible that . . ."

"The lady has a very just motive or reason for complaint," Don Teódulo interrupted again. "But there are cases in which it is not possible to . . ."

"And what business is it of yours?" asked Don Casimiro irritably.

Don Teódulo lowered his head, and they all kept looking at one another amid an increasingly uncomfortable silence. Finally Sister Lupe came in.

"Mother Fermina," she said, "the gentlemen you were expecting are here now."

Mother Fermina rose and went out, followed by Don Teódulo. They both reentered after a short while, accompanied by two uniformed policemen, one of whom was a captain.

"What is this?" asked Don Casimiro, rising.

"The police, or public safety force," Don Teódulo answered softly, with a timid smile on his lips.

"And what are the police doing here?" shouted Don Casimiro. "There has been enough delay, Mother Fermina; let our dear sister's body be released to us. We are leaving!"

"At present," said the captain, "a doctor is examining her corpse."

"Is *what?*" cried Don Casimiro.

"An accusation has been made: it appears that the lady was murdered . . ."

"But she died of natural causes . . ." interrupted one of the nephews.

"Exactly," said Don Teódulo. "Of natural causes — a blood clot in her heart."

"I don't understand all this," Doña María interrupted. "Casimiro, tell those policemen to leave, and we shall go . . ."

"Let's go," said Don Casimiro, getting up. "It appears that everyone agrees that Leocadia died of natural causes."

"That is so: the lady died or passed away from natural causes; there is nothing more natural than a clot. Unfortunately, this one was caused or brought on by a foreign or artificial substance, which can and should be considered homicide or murder . . ."

"Good Lord!" cried Doña María. "But who could have . . ."

"That is precisely what we wish to discover or find out, and I believe that one of you was . . ."

"Do you dare to insinuate that one of us murdered Leocadia?" exclaimed Don Casimiro with such deep indignation that the tips of his mustache quivered.

"That is what I dared to say — and not insinuate, as you put it. One of those present, disguising himself as an intern in this hospital or sanitarium, went into the room occupied by the patient, Doña Leocadia, now deceased — God rest her soul — and killed or murdered her . . ."

"You did it, Juan," interrupted Doña María, pointing to one of the nephews. He stood up, pale and blear-eyed.

"You're all crazy," he said. "If someone killed the old woman he did the right thing; but it wasn't I."

Clara, too, arose: "Don't say that, Juan; she was our aunt . . ."

"She was a stingy old woman," Juan insisted. "But I didn't kill her. I don't know who killed her, or how."

"He wasn't the one," said Clara. "He was with me all morning in the garden, and now in here."

"The two of them together must have killed her," shouted María. "They are both poor, and knew Leocadia was going to disinherit them on account of the scandalous life they lead, the same as Ambrosio . . ."

"Be quiet, Aunt María," interrupted Ambrosio. "You are shouting too much. Besides, just remember that you detested the old woman, too, and said many times that she was stingy, and that . . ."

"I'm sorry to interrupt this tender family scene," said Don Teódulo, "but I believe or consider it appropriate to pass on to other matters. First it is essential or necessary to know what each one of you was doing from the point or moment when you found out that the lady had been operated upon successfully until I saw you all together or gathered in the visitors' room. We shall begin or start with the ladies; kindly tell us, Doña María."

"What I was doing is none of your business!"

"Please, madam," exclaimed the captain. "Kindly answer. A murder has been committed here . . ."

"When they brought my beloved sister from the operating room I wanted to stay with her, but Mother Fermina said no, and made me wait in the visitors' room; this action of hers surprised me a great deal."

"The patient had given orders to that effect," said Mother Fermina.

"I understand. And you, Don Casimiro? What did you do?"

"I waited a bit in the visitors' room with my sister, and then went out to take a short stroll."

"And you, Don Juan?"

"I went with Clara for a walk and a smoke in the garden."

"That's right," said Clara. "I was with him. We had a lot to talk about and we invited Ambrosio, but he preferred to find a comfortable chair and sleep."

"Did you have something special to talk about or discuss?" asked Don Teódulo.

"Nothing in particular," Juan replied.

"I told them this morning," interrupted Don Casimiro, "that Leocadia intended to disinherit them by changing her will. They probably went out to discuss that, and took advantage of the opportunity to murder the poor sick woman."

"That's true; Uncle Casimiro did tell us that," agreed Clara, "but it never entered our heads to murder our aunt. It is true that she didn't like us, but she had much less liking for her brother and sister here; they always reminded her of vultures, she told me one day . . ."

"Clara!" roared María. "I forbid you to talk like that!"

"Please, madam," Don Teódulo interrupted. "Now, you say or state, Don Casimiro, that Doña Leocadia told you before her death or demise that she intended to change her will so as to disinherit or leave nothing to these young people."

"Precisely," agreed Don Casimiro.

"Well, permit me to tell you that you are lying or not telling the truth. No — please do not interrupt me. What you have stated is truly absurd or foolish: if the lady intended to change her last will or testament, she would have done it before undergoing an operation that placed her life in danger. Now then, I beg you all to hear or listen to me in silence. The lady's death was due to an intravenous injection of air that was given to her by one of you. I already know that only one person entered or went into the patient's room; that in order to enter without arousing suspicion that person stole Pedro's gown and mask; that the hypodermic syringe was carried in that person's pocket, since there wasn't any in the patient's room or sleeping quarters; that the injection of air was put into her vein, causing an instant embolism or clot; that the syringe was put back into the person's pocket, but that nervousness prevented the replacement of the needle into its little case where the point would not prick, so it was thrown out the window; and that this individual or person left the room, discarded the gown someplace in the corridor where Sister Lupe, who was on duty, could not see. But the mask was not discarded, and there can be only one reason for its having been carried off: there was a mark on the mask that indicated who had used it. Only two people could have left a mark that stained or soiled the mask: Clara, who uses lipstick, or Don Casimiro, who colors or dyes his moustache. . . ."

"This is absurd!" cried Don Casimiro.

"Having reduced our suspects or possible culprits to two," continued Don Teódulo without paying any attention to them, "we need make only a few brief remarks. Sister Lupe has told me that she saw a male intern go in. How does one recognize at a quick glance the legs of members of the male sex? By the trousers they wear. Therefore the murderer or slayer was wearing trousers. Clara could have worn them or put them on, but they would have had to be her brother Juan's, who in this case would be her accomplice. Don Casimiro needed to make no change at all. On the other hand, the gown would have been much too large for Clara, while it would have been more or less the right size or fit for Don Casimiro.

"But in addition to all these pieces of evidence against Don Casimiro, there is one of even greater weight. I have said that the murderer hid the mask because he had left a stain on it, either from the tint or lipstick a lady uses on her mouth, or from the dye or coloring Don Casimiro uses on his moustache. Now then, the murderer must have realized that he was going to leave that mark or stain. If it had been a woman she would have cleaned or wiped the lipstick off her mouth; but Don Casimiro could not do that because it would have been difficult for him to stain or dye his moustache again here. Therefore I accuse Don Casimiro of the murder of his sister, and request the captain to search him. In one of his pockets will be found a new hypodermic syringe with bloodstains, but without a trace of any other substance, together with the mask soiled or stained by the dye from his moustache or whiskers."

Don Casimiro kept still while the captain searched his pockets. In one of them he found what Don Teódulo had indicated, and placed them on the table. After Don Casimiro had left the room between two policemen, Don Teódulo approached Mother Fermina and said to her, "Now I can take leave of you. I beg you to accept this rosary, and to offer up a prayer or supplication for me. Good afternoon, ladies and gentlemen."

"One moment," said the captain, detaining Don Teódulo. "There are many details about this affair that I do not understand, and I beg you to explain them to me. For example, how did you find out it was a question of murder and not death from natural causes?"

"There is nothing easier or simpler. First that needle fell into my hands; it was God's will that it should fall into mine, so that this crime would not go unpunished. Then I found out that Pedro had lost his gown and found it again, but not the missing mask. After that came the news or information about the lady's death. The doctor said it seemed strange to him because the lady — or deceased lady — was perfectly all right when she left the operating room. All these things set me to thinking, so much so that I took the needle to the laboratory, where they told me nothing had been injected with it. Then I began to conjecture how the lady could have been murdered.

"There was only one means or method: an injection of air, which brought on the embolism that in its turn caused her death or demise, apparently from completely natural causes. To eliminate any doubt, I asked whether the body showed marks or indications of having received, while still alive, an intravenous injection. Sister Lupe stated or affirmed that there was such a mark, and moreover, that the injection that made or caused it has been administered unskillfully. This confirmed my suspicions, especially when I discovered that no intern had entered the patient's room or sleeping quarters after the operation. Without doubt, I had arrived at an accurate or correct deduction. Doña Leocadia had been murdered. The missing mask gave me the clue to the identity of the murderer or slayer."

"Thank you, Don Teódulo; now I understand," said the captain.

Gonzalo
Mazas Garbayo
1904 -

was born and raised in the rural province of Las Villas in Cuba. After studying in the United States and at the University of Havana, he became a Doctor of Medicine at the age of twenty-three. He has earned a splendid reputation as a physician, and has published medical treatises of great merit.

While still a medical student, Dr. Mazas Garbayo published his first volume of verse: Poemas del hospital *(1925). He has since written other poetry, and in 1945 published his collected verse in a greatly expanded volume,* Las sombras conmovidas *(Sorrowing Shadows). But it is his work in the field of the short story that is of greatest interest to us here.*

In 1930, he and Pablo de la Torriente Brau (with whom he starred as a football player on the Havana team) jointly published a collection called Batey: Cuentos cubanos, *a series of twenty-one tales that present a broad cross-section of Cuban life — students, city dwellers, the* guajiros *(Cuban farmers), and sugar mill workers. This collection received high praise from literary critics throughout the Spanish-speaking world, particularly in Spain and in Mexico. The story translated here — El valle — presents a grim but all-too-true picture of life in the sugar cane regions of Cuba, and for that matter in many of the other sugar growing islands of the Caribbean. The bohíos, squalid shacks usually made of palm tree lumber, are the symbol of rural poverty and disease that Dr. Mazas Garbayo looks at with a clinical eye.*

The utter hopelessness of the individual farmer's own economic situation in a one-crop region drives him to violence as a desperate but futile protest against the more efficient working of the land in large units — in this case by a corporation. Just how the picture may change in contemporary Cuba remains to be seen.

THE VALLEY

* * *

Hoofbeats were heard galloping furiously, and suddenly a horseman rode into view over the brow of a hill. He was whipping his mount fiercely, and drawing blood from its flanks with his sharp spurs. The inhabitants of the house peered out the door. From within, a voice asked who it was.

"It's Manuel," they answered.

Manuel Sánchez was a farmer. His strong muscles rippled visibly beneath his short jacket; he wore a broad brimmed hat, and the merciless riding crop hung from his waist. Manuel jumped down from his horse and went into the cabin, stooping as he passed through the door. As he dropped down on a stool and took off his hat, his black hair stuck to his sweaty forehead.

His wife and children gathered around him—five dirty, swarthy boys with swollen stomachs. The eldest must have been about eight years old. Manuel's emaciated wife, with obvious signs of malaria, lacked any youthful vitality in her face, which was lined with premature wrinkles; beneath her narrow forehead, her eyes were dull and listless. When she spoke she seemed to be mumbling some unintelligible prayer in her slow and tired voice; and when she opened her mouth, the two remaining teeth stood like sentinels at the opening of a cave.

In one corner sat a paralyzed man, upon whose thighs rested a pair of crutches as the symbol of all helplessness. He was Manuel's father. Greyhaired and wrinkled, he had been living with his son since bad attacks of fever left him in that condition. He was no longer able to go out into the fields and manage a plow, or to call the stray cattle in a strong voice; and there in his wheel chair, a broken man, a kind of useless hulk, he bemoaned his fate. In a voice that quavered with fear he asked Manuel, who was drinking a cup of coffee, "What news do you have?"

"Bad," Manuel replied. "The bank manager didn't want to see me. Through his secretary he informed me that he would make no further extensions, and that legal steps are being taken to foreclose the mortgage on our lands. I don't know what to do or where to turn."

Slowly he folded his arms. His eyes flashed like lightning, and a curse thundered against the roof of his mouth. The boys, sensing the threat of a storm, stopped their games and shouting; one by one they took shelter beneath the table, where two black dogs, full of mud and vermin, growled at the unwelcome interruption to their sleep.

Outside, it began to rain. The drops of water pattered on the palm leaf roof and began to turn the ground to mud. The wife came in through the kitchen door, carrying tin plates and dishes. The boys fell hungrily upon the scanty food: dried beef, rice and vegetables. Their fingers made handy forks, and their teeth munched noisily.

Manuel watched the scene in silence as he smoked. And his father, from his corner, with the crutches across his useless legs, looked through tearful eyes at what was going on about him, and asked himself sadly why God did not take the breath of life from his crippled body. . . .

2

THE FARM WHERE THEY LIVED was set in the middle of a valley, surrounded by other farms whose owners were in exactly the same financial situation. All those lands were surrounded by mountains. A river, whose swift, green current was fed by waters from the whole district, left the valley through a mountain pass whose cliffs rose smooth and insurmountable.

Fields of sugar cane swayed softly with the breeze. Palms, crowned with decorative tufts, rose on straight, tall trunks, and a profusion of tropical trees cast their pools of shadow upon those lands, seared by the blazing sun.

The fields were handed down from one generation to the next, and were the only legacy of those rude, simple country folk, who clung to the land where their forebears had died and their children were born. Every day at the break of dawn plows were busy opening furrows as the voices of the farmers rang out like a reveille calling to the animals.

With no distractions, the farm folk married early and burdened themselves with an endless number of children.

Only on holidays did they stay up a little longer: a few hours after dark it was rare to see a kerosene lamp shining through the cracks in the cabins. Early in the morning people began to stir. Burning wood crackled in fireplaces made of upright bricks with two iron bars across the top; in the smoke-filled shacks, water for coffee bubbled noisily in tin pots.

Manuel had spent his whole life in those surroundings. Sometimes he had enough money to live decently, other times very little; but he was always hard-working and energetic.

A very bad year came: a storm and flood destroyed the crop. By some stupendous feats of budget balancing he managed to cover his losses. But his bankbook at the bottom of his trunk no longer showed any savings, and his yokes of oxen dwindled substantially.

"As long as we have our health, what difference do failures and misfortunes make?" he said. Smiling hopefully, he set to work again. And the owners of the neighboring sugar plantations did likewise.

But the next year was bad again. The price of sugar dropped unexpectedly. The owners of the mill where they crushed his cane could not pay him in full, and another company took over the plant, whose stacks sent a column of thick, black smoke straight up to join the sky. On the last day of operations, the whistle blew mournfully, like a doleful prayer for the dead.

To pay their debts and have something to begin work again, they borrowed money from the bank in the nearby town, a branch of the greedy octopus in Havana whose tentacles stretch the whole length of the island.

Two terrible years went by. Their losses mounted, and it was impossible to pay. Now foreclosure proceedings were being instituted in the town court.

3

THAT NIGHT lights burned in all the cabins. Dawn found the farmers pale, sleepless and thoughtful.

At eight o'clock in the morning several soldiers and a sergeant, accompanying the judge and the bank officials, appeared in the valley. The farmers were ordered in the name of the law to vacate those lands. A ripple of rebellion caused their hands to tighten upon their sharp machetes. The soldiers raised their rifles. The farmers looked at one another, and their hands dropped to their sides, motionless, useless. The abandonment of their lands began. . . .

Manuel's wife, with the smallest child in her arms, rode on the horse behind his father, who could hardly hold himself on. The rest took up the journey on foot. Hatred, resentment, the desire for revenge, seared his soul like a cruel, white-hot branding iron.

4

MANUEL SOUGHT SHELTER in the house of a friend. Shortly afterward, his father died broken-hearted, and two of the boys followed him to the grave. Misfortune showed no mercy toward the family.

Manuel worked at anything and everything. One day he got a job as a watchman at a nearby quarry. He had the keys to the store of tools and explosives, and spent the nights smoking cigarettes to fight off drowsiness.

Meanwhile the valley had undergone great changes. The new owners put up big, barrack-like housing for the farmhands, harnessed the river current, and built an electric power plant to drive all kinds of machinery.

One day Manuel mysteriously disappeared from his job, taking with him the horse of one of the workers.

5

THE EARLY MORNING HOURS. Starlight shone down upon the valley, revealing the white walls of the sugar mills. A man on horseback plunged into the river and drew close to the side of the narrow mountain pass. He dug out some earth, and placed something into the hole he had made. He struck a match, and its sparkle pierced the darkness. . . . Then he made his horse swim along with the river current, and soon the echo of his furious galloping followed close behind him like a pack of hounds. . . .

A vivid flash filled the valley, and a frightful explosion

roared through the night. The walls of the mountain pass hurtled toward each other and fell into the river. The waters began then to pour out of the river bed. Bursting forth in their fury, they swept away everything in their path. In the darkness there was a horrible confusion of shouts and curses of men, mixed with the bellowing of animals. Later, only the gurgle of the waters, rising, rising. . . .

Daylight disclosed the flooded valley: floating in the waters were men, animals, wreckage of all kinds.

On a mountain top, standing in the stirrups of his horse, a scowling, tragic man, his eyes aglow with intense satisfaction, looked down upon the catastrophe beneath him. It was like an offering to some bloodthirsty divinity, for at that moment he was the incarnation of the god of supreme vengeance. That man was Manuel Sánchez.

His horse gave a whinny that was borne by the wind and wafted along with the river current.

Smiling satanically, he lit a cigar and began to descend the mountain slowly, down a trail that was drenched in sunlight. . . .

Enrique Serpa

1899 -

is one of Cuba's outstanding contemporary writers.
He is a perceptive and sensitive interpreter of his
native city — Havana — where his work as a newspaperman has twice won him awards in journalism
equivalent to our Pulitzer Prize.

Serpa's writing, however, is not limited to report-
ing on the Cuban scene. He has travelled widely
throughout Spanish America and has written several
series of articles on political and social conditions
in other Latin lands. In addition to these, he has
published two volumes of poetry and several works
of literary criticism. Serpa's novel Contrabando
(1938) won the Ministry of Education prize for its
vigorous and colorful description of smuggling off
the Cuban coast. The ocean itself and the motley
collection of human types around Havana's harbor
are the real protagonists of this powerful novel of
contemporary Cuban life.

In the field of the short story Serpa has given us
two splendid collections: Felisa y yo (Felisa and I)

in 1937, and Noche de fiesta (Festive Night) *in 1951. It is from the former that the story translated here has been selected.*

The description of the guerrilla band fighting the Spaniards in 1898 is equally applicable to the conditions that have obtained during the many revolutions that have beset Cuba in the twentieth century. The War of 1868 mentioned in the story refers to the struggle which began then and lasted for ten long years while Cuba tried unsuccessfully to gain her independence from Spain. Serpa gives us a revealing picture of the very personal nature of the military relationship between a guerrilla leader and his men. The loose confederation of many of these private bands — the members of which have a strong personal loyalty to their chief — is what makes up an insurgent "army" in many Latin American revolutions. And if the revolution is won, the problem of which chief is to be supreme all too tragically often leads to further civil strife.

AGAINST REGULATIONS

✳   ✳   ✳

WHEN THEY TOLD HIM the news, Captain Agramonte
— called "Big Brother" by the rebels because of his
kindness to his soldiers — kept silent, sunk in sorrowful
surprise. His face, usually pleasant, intelligent, and gentle,
had taken on the blank expression of someone who is trying
in vain to unravel a mystery. He stayed silent for some time.

"Are you sure?" he asked the sergeant who had told him
the news.

"He makes no effort to conceal it. He swears that the
first chance he gets he is going over to the Spaniards. But
I don't think the boys are going to give him time. When
he least expects it they are going to lop off his head. Castillo has spent the whole morning saying atrocious things
about traitors who desert. I imagine he's just waiting for
Hernández to answer, so as to cut off his head. . . ."

"Tell Hernández to report to me."

When he found himself alone the captain thought about
the attitude of Hernández Trujillo and the consequences
it could bring. The case was unusual enough to upset him;
it seemed absurd. Perhaps a misinterpretation, possibly a
word spoken without thinking. . . .

Until that moment he had had blind confidence in the
loyalty of his men, who used to charge into the face of
death with a smile on their lips and a bright dream of
liberty in their hearts. But he realized that the situation
was growing worse every day. Of the 180 men that formed
his company the month before, only 66 were left. And no
longer could they even be called riflemen, as they were

several weeks ago: among the lot of them they could scarcely muster thirty rifles and three hundred bullets. They were all walking around half naked and without shoes. There were some who were armed only with a dented machete stuck into a crude palm leaf scabbard hanging from a piece of raw leather about the waist.

Moreover, food was scarce. The day before they had tasted only guava and scrub pineapple, which, when eaten in abundance, causes painful sores in the mouth and makes the tongue bleed.

Under such conditions one desertion could be fatal because it would weaken the faith the rebels needed to endure the harsh trials to which they were being subjected. And the case was even more serious because it involved Hernández Trujillo, one of the six men who had started out with him when he decided to join the revolution.

Captain Agramonte's thoughts were interrupted by the arrival of a young man of twenty-four, with large eyes, a firm chin, and tight-pressed lips — Hernández Trujillo — who inquired:

"You sent for me?"

"Yes. We need to have a talk," answered Captain Agramonte, looking at him enigmatically. And pointing out a hammock made of hemp bags he added:

"Sit down."

"Thanks. I'm all right this way," said Hernández in a low voice as he rested his back against a *ceiba* tree and put his hands into his pockets in an insolent manner.

"Listen. They tell me you want to surrender. Is it true?" asked Captain Agramonte, looking Hernández Trujillo straight in the eye.

The latter tried to meet the stern gaze of the speaker, but quickly lowered his eyes.

"They have not deceived you."

"Take your hands out of your pockets when I speak to you!"

Hernández Trujillo obeyed, although reluctantly.

"Then you've made up your mind to do this?"

"Yes. I can't go on this way. This isn't living, or fighting, or anything! Look at the way I am!"

The soldier spread his arms with a gesture of hopelessness, letting the captain see the rags that covered part of his body. His short-sleeved shirt was completely in tatters, and his trousers didn't even reach his knees.

"Why, you don't look so bad at all . . . you even have shoes! I wish all the boys could say the same. You're almost a dandy! But then," the captain joked, with bitter compassion, "I understand. Our life is hard, and we march too close to death. It isn't pleasant to rub elbows with danger; it's nicer to stroll with the ladies. And it's more enjoyable to strut in a salon than to plod wearily through the jungles. Caramba! There are some fellows who simply can't take this life, and we mustn't criticize them. What the devil! Maybe we should feel sorry for their girlish frailty."

Hernández Trujillo's cheeks flushed as if he had been slapped.

"You have no right to say that! I've been with you from the beginning, and I've always been a good soldier. I've never hesitated to charge and expose myself to danger. And the proof of it is that you have recommended me for a corporal's stripes."

"Yes, but that was before. Not now. It seems to me that now danger frightens you. Just when the revolution needs us most, you want to quit. A rooster that runs from the cockfight at the first thrust! I'm sorry about all this, really sorry. If I could, I'd try to find a way to keep you happy. I'd give anything to be able to make you a present of a nice pair of patent leather shoes, a form-fitting suit and a top hat. And you wouldn't mind a bit of powder, eh?"

"Bah! Go ahead and make fun of me! That won't stop me from leaving!"

"I'm not even going to try, my boy. We need men who are completely dedicated. Only with a pure soul and willing heart does one take to the jungle, which is a temple of sacrifice and not a bed of roses. In this crucible gold becomes purer, and lead melts down. What good would I be doing by stopping you? Just wasting food. I don't like that arrangement. I don't want to stop you, not in the slightest. You know that I could, don't you?"

Receiving no reply, Captain Agramonte continued:

"No, my boy, not at all. Let them hang you somewhere else. The desertion of useless men will be a stimulus for the good ones. From the shame of the desertions we shall draw strength to win. No one will be able to say that Agramonte's boys killed a defenseless man, even though that man was thinking of deserting and the code of honor demanded his death. On the other hand, we thank you for what you have done for Cuba, and we shall not forget that at one time you were one of our good soldiers. . . . When are you going to surrender?"

"If I'm not hanged, as soon as I can. At the first opportunity."

"Oh? You can do it this very day, if you wish. We have four horses left; you can take one."

"Are you serious?"

"And how serious! When do you want to leave?"

Hernández Trujillo did not answer. The captain's words cut through his flesh and seared his heart like a burst of molten metal. He had foreseen and expected a violent scene, during which he would have run the risk of a bul-

let or a drumhead court martial concluding in a macabre
dance of death. And suddenly he encountered something
completely unexpected. The captain's attitude disturbed
him; his generosity moved him. His words, harsh but vi-
brating with nobility and patriotism — — sarcastic at times,
but filled with undefined tenderness and affectionate pity
— had a strange and disturbing effect upon him, a mix-
ture of remorse and eagerness to prove that his courage was
not weakening.

Moreover, the decision he had reached was not really
dictated by his own conscience; indeed, it seemed like a
thing of the Devil! He had behaved like an automaton in
this matter, obeying an impulse that he could not succeed
in defining clearly, and against which his own will was of
no avail. At first the idea of handing himself over to the
Spanish authorities had made him smile — so impossible
was it — and he asked himself the question, "What would
they do to me?" Later he thought about it again more seriously. And finally it had become a veritable obsession that
kept his frayed nerves as taut as wires.

He tried to overcome the idea, but this was worse: the
more he tried to stifle it the more intensely he felt it rise
again. There were times when the obsession became un-
bearable. On such occasions he felt deathly pains clutching
at his throat and heart, and a trickle of cold sweat bathed
his brow. He would sink into a desperate mood of terror
and shame which caused him to flush when even thinking about it, and obliged him to hide from his comrades
for fear they might see him in that condition and read his
thoughts. At last, wanting to prove to himself that it was
not the fear of death that was prompting him to desert, he
had told the other rebels about his plans, which could
mean a hangman's noose for his neck. And suddenly, instead of the risk he had sought, he found the kindness and

pity of the Big Brother. It was enough to make him die of shame! The earth should have swallowed him up right there on the spot!

In view of the fact that Hernández Trujillo wasn't saying a word in reply, Captain Agramonte told him:

"Come on! Don't think about it any more! You can leave this very day."

Now the vows he had taken upon joining the revolution rose in Hernández Trujillo's memory; the chaste kiss of his fiancée, pale and lovely, who bit her lips in order not to cry, because she was afraid she might sadden the leave-taking of her beloved, who made her proud of his courage; the blessing of his old mother, who at the moment of his departure remembered his father, who had also fought for Cuba in the Revolution of 1868. . . .

While Hernández Trujillo was musing, Captain Agramonte took off his own coarsely patched shirt, stained with red earth, and his battered straw sombrero. He held out both articles in his hands, and on his face was the hesitant expression of one who is offering a gift that is too poor. Then he put them into Hernández Trujillo's hands as he said apologetically:

"Take them, my boy. Please forgive their bad condition. . . . You will look a little more presentable when you surrender."

Hernández Trujillo's face broke into an expression of surprise.

"What, captain? And you . . . ?"

"Don't worry. My men won't blush when they see me without a shirt. And this way my chest will be more open to the enemy's bullets."

He stopped a moment, and then continued:

"I am going to ask you a favor. It is unnecessary for the Spaniards to find out that we are short of weapons, too.

Take my revolver. I can get along with just a machete."

Hernández Trujillo wanted to speak, but his words came out as broken, meaningless sounds. At last he was able to sob, "Captain . . . captain . . . No!"

His head bowed beneath the weight of remorse and emotion. For several minutes he remained that way; finally he raised his eyes, moist with tears:

"Captain, I've been a coward and a traitor! May Cuba forgive me! But I swear to you that in the next battle I'll redeem myself. I . . . I . . ."

And he said no more. He made an about face to march off, and advanced several paces, staggering like a drunken man. But the captain's voice stopped him short:

"Caramba! Not like that! Let me embrace you!"

The two men's chests came close in a strong embrace, and Francisco Hernández Trujillo, who had faced death time and again without flinching, begain to cry like a child on the Big Brother's shoulder. . . .

Cayetano Coll y Toste

1850-1930

was born in Puerto Rico and received his early education there. His family was of Catalan origin, and he
went to Barcelona to earn his M.D. degree, for
Puerto Rico was still a Spanish possession in those
days. The University of Puerto Rico was not founded
until 1902. Although Dr. Coll y Toste practiced his
profession throughout his long life and wrote several
medical treatises (he published a work on yellow
fever in 1895, while Dr. Carlos Finlay was working
on the same problem in Cuba), his great love was
the history and folklore of his island.

It should be remembered that of all the areas of
the New World, the Caribbean was under Spanish
cultural influence the longest. Columbus' landings
and early settlements were in the islands, and the first
colonization of the American mainland did not take
place until a quarter of a century later, when Cortés
left Cuba to conquer Mexico in 1519. Moreover, the
flag of Spain flew in the Caribbean until 1898, three
quarters of a century after the other Spanish Amer-

ican republics had been founded. It is not surprising, therefore, that Coll y Toste, who was a Spanish subject for more than half his life, should emphasize the colonial period in his many historical works, even in those published in the twentieth century.

When the United States took possession of Puerto Rico the doctor's attitude — like that of most of the older generation — was one of brave acceptance of the new, with warm nostalgia for the old. Under the new government Coll y Toste wrote several valuable volumes on the history of education and social conditions on the island. He was named official historian of Puerto Rico in 1913, and from 1914 to 1927 directed the Boletín histórico de Puerto Rico, which is valuable source material today.

The story we have translated here is taken from one of his collections of traditions and legends of Puerto Rico (Tradiciones y leyendas puertorriqueñas), published in Barcelona in 1928. Coll y Toste is, in a sense, the Ricardo Palma of his native land: his tales are woven around such items as old sayings, decaying fortresses, religious relics, and picturesque place names. The pirate island in this story lies just off the south coast of Puerto Rico. The student will note the admixture of races and nationalities, so typical of the Caribbean area.

THE PIRATE'S TREASURE

❋   ❋   ❋

JOSÉ ALMEIDA was a young Portuguese, twenty-five years of age. He was tall, strong, and swarthy, with a thick, black beard, flashing eyes, full lips, and bushy eyebrows upon a high forehead topped by a heavy head of hair. He was a fine, handsome type of Iberian, with a trace of Berber blood.

He had been born in Lisbon. After the death of his fiancée in Oporto, where they worked for a large firm that sold excellent wines, he decided to emigrate to America to forget his misfortune. The Oporto concern had good connections in Curaçao, and he determined to set out for there. He bore letters of recommendation addressed to Souza and Company.

Senhor Souza liked the look of his compatriot, and employed him in his warehouse. The energetic and intelligent young Portuguese, whose handwriting was very good, soon advanced to bookkeeper and commercial correspondent. Within a year he was a member of the firm because of the good results obtained through his financial advice to the head of the business.

One afternoon Almeida felt like visiting the other side of the city of Curaçao, and went there for a ride. As he landed from the ferry boat he saw a refreshment stand operated by a Dutch woman who was part Negro, and went over to buy some fruit. A moment later a haughty young lady came up and asked the Dutch woman for some guava jelly tarts. Almeida said to the vendor, "Serve this young lady ahead of me: first, because she is a lady, and second, because she is so lovely."

"Thank you, sir, for your courtesy," she said as she beamed upon the young Portuguese with a melting look that overwhelmed him. The young lady picked up the tarts, and with a gracious bow and a slight toss of her head walked off. Almeida followed her with his eyes, and then, carrying his fruit with him, kept watching her from a distance. He saw her go into a house opposite a Protestant church. Having marked the spot in his mind, he left that part of town.

The next day he returned and began to walk up and down in front of the unknown lady's home. It was a modest little house. The lovely young woman came out on the balcony; emboldened, he greeted her. She returned the greeting and Almeida, hat in hand, approached in order to speak to her. The lady spoke first:

"You don't come from around here?"

"I am Portuguese, lovely lady."

"And do you value your life?"

"Of course! Why do you ask me that?"

"Because I am a married woman, and my husband is extremely hot-tempered. If he finds you around this neighborhood he will thrash you within an inch of your life."

"That's if I let him!"

"Ask in Curaçao about Miguel Igartúa — he works at Ulibarri Company foundry — and heed what they tell you. You are a handsome young man who has obviously fallen in love with me. You come too late: the fortress has been captured. Pray God to let you find a fine young girl to your liking somewhere else. Good-bye. . . ."

And she went inside. Almeida began to walk away. He felt that his face was on fire, as if he had been slapped by her frank words. As he got on the boat he muttered to himself, "That haughty woman will be mine . . . I swear it!"

2

THE FOLLOWING MORNING he went to the foundry of Ulibarri and Company, and walked boldly into the big shop. A brawny young man came out to take care of him. Almeida said:

"Can I get this lock fixed here?"

"No, sir; here we make only iron castings. You can find what you want three doors down; a locksmith lives there."

"Are you the owner of this foundry?"

"No, sir; I am an employe of the firm. You are new in these parts, it seems."

"I am Portuguese — a partner in Souza and Company. My name is José Almeida. Your servant, sir."

"Well, my name is Miguel Igartúa, and I live on the other side of the city. At your service, sir."

3

ALMEIDA WENT HOME. Now he was on the track. He made discreet inquiries about his man, and obtained full information. That afternoon he went across to the other side of town and went into a tavern, in accordance with the notes he had jotted down in his book. He ordered a dish of tripe and a half bottle of port wine.

In a short while Igartúa came into the little restaurant. He saw the Portuguese, who was enjoying his food, and in a resounding voice, brisk and booming, said as he approached the table:

"Hello, there! So you like tripe, too, just as I do! May I sit down at your table?"

"The pleasure is mine!" answered the Portuguese, who added: "Have a glass of wine from my country."

Igartúa drained down the glass of port wine that Almeida offered him, and after thanking him, said, "I'll wash down my meal with Catalan wine from the monastery, and afterward we'll have a bit of Basque cider, from my country."

"Are you a Basque?"

"I came from there, and so did my wife."

"You are married?"

"To a girl from my town, sweet as a peach and gay as a nightingale."

They finished dinner and went into the sitting room. Igartúa invited Almeida to play dominoes with him and some friends who were already there at the table, and Almeida accepted with pleasure.

Every afternoon they would get together for a dish of tripe with port wine and Basque cider; then they would play dominoes until nine o'clock. The two men became fast friends.

One day Igartúa invited Almeida for lunch, to taste some codfish cooked in Basque style by his wife; Almeida accepted.

When the appointed Sunday came, the Portuguese arrived at the Basque's house fifteen minutes ahead of time. The door was opened by the Basque girl, who was surprised to find the Portuguese there and stepped back two paces in alarm. She said to him in a tone of rebuke:

"My husband is not at home; please wait for him outside."

"Why? Let's go out on the balcony, and from there we can watch for him."

"You are looking for trouble, and you're certainly going

to find it. I know that you are good friends, and that you have tripe together each evening and play dominoes. But if Miguel suspects that you are in love with me, he'll stick a knife into your hide and leave you a corpse with the first thrust. And you wouldn't be the first he killed in a jealous rage, because he has already brought two unfortunate and stubborn young men to an untimely end."

"I'm very sorry about that, señora, but I adore you with all my heart, and neither Miguel nor his patron saint can cause me to change that feeling."

"All right! Adore me all you want, for every woman likes to be attractive to fine young men; but don't look at me across the table. Act indifferent, for if my husband suspects that you are fond of me — alas! — you are as good as dead. And it's really a shame, because you could make any other woman very happy. Ah! Here comes Miguel! Walk far out on the balcony so he can see you."

Igartúa arrived right on time, embraced his wife, and shook hands with his friend. He sat down on a wicker rocking chair, and exclaimed:

"I'm famished. Let's see, wife; please bring us some olives, a few nice slices of sausage, and glasses for sherry as an appetizer. Then — as soon as you can — the codfish."

The two friends ate heartily when Igartúa's wife served the special dish. Almeida did not even look at her. The Basque said to him:

"Why, you're forgetting to thank my wife for the fine, tasty meal she fixed for us!"

"How can I thank her, my friend, if you haven't yet introduced me to her?"

"You're right! Come over, Alida Blanca. This gentleman's name is Almeida; he is a member of the firm of Souza and Company, and a good friend of mine."

"Señora, I am delighted to meet you, and I congratulate

you on your skill in the domestic arts. I wish you all kinds of success. Please consider me at your service."

He said all this without even looking at her. Then he immediately went to the hatrack, took his hat, and said to Igartúa:

"I forgot to finish the mail and take the letters to the post office. I really must go. This evening I'll drop by for a short visit."

Igartúa and his wife went out on the balcony to watch him as he left. When he was quite far away, Miguel said to Alida Blanca:

"This Almeida is an extraordinary fellow. He never flirts with the girls who come into the tavern, and he doesn't like his friends to say anything bad about women. He always tells them: 'God made women for men to adore'."

"Well, he's right!"

"Is he? Well, he never even looked at you — not even when he complimented you on the codfish you cooked."

"How do you know he didn't look at me?"

"Because I was watching to see if he liked you."

"Well, that's certainly a nice way to act! And suppose he did like me — what were you going to do?"

"Never ask him to my house again. And if he was really interested in you, I'd slit his hide — as you know full well I can do."

4

AS ALMEIDA GOT into the boat he said to himself, "That lovely woman really likes me. How pretty she looked today! I realized that she liked me by the way she looked at me the first time; today I'm sure of it. A woman who compares two men soon decides. Her husband has red hairs sticking out on his face, a squint in his left eye, and his body is a grotesque bundle of flesh. . . ."

That night in his room he began to stride up and down, saying to himself: "My mind is made up. That woman will be mine! But I have to get rid of that man who stands in the way. There's the problem!"

Apparently he found the solution, for he got into bed and tucked under the covers. And as he dropped off to sleep he exclaimed, "She'll be mine! She'll be mine!"

5

"SENHOR SOUZA, you know I have been working in your firm for over two years. I need to take a trip to forget my troubles. According to my calculations, I have saved up 3,000 pesos, deposited in the company's funds. May I have them?"

"At once, if you like."

"I'd like to invest it with a shipowner."

"Captain Perico Trinidad told me this morning that he needed exactly 3,000 pesos. He has his schooner *Relámpago* mortgaged to the moneylender Gaigal, who is charging him three per cent interest per month."

"Where can I see Captain Trinidad?"

"He told me he'd be back here at five this afternoon."

6

"CAPTAIN PERICO, my partner has the 3,000 pesos you need."

"Please call him in."

"What interest would you ask, Senhor Almeida, for the 3,000 pesos?"

"None. I want to go to sea. Let me become your partner."

"Very well, then. You will be the cargo officer, and I the captain of the *Relámpago*. I'll give you a bill of sale for half ownership of the craft. We'll divide the profits equally."

"Agreed. When do you weigh anchor?"

"This afternoon with the breeze. The business can be concluded today."

"And where are you bound for?"

"To the Turcas Islands, to get some salt."

"Then I'm going to pack my gear. Bring the notary, and get Senhor Souza to hand over the money to you."

7

FOR SIX MONTHS Almeida kept nursing his plan to make the Basque girl his own. One morning when they were off the Cuban coast he said to his companion:

"Captain Trinidad, in this inter-colonial trade the earnings aren't very high. This schooner is very fast, and strongly made. Let's arm her as a privateer and cruise around pirating."

"I'm no good for that business; I don't know a thing about it," replied the captain.

"But I do! My father was a privateer against the English, and as a boy I went along on his ship. It's a great life, full of adventures and thrills. Let me have the ship fitted out as a strongly armed privateer, and soon you'll be rich — very rich."

"Well, you take over. From now on you're the captain and I'm second in command on board here when it comes to matters of piracy."

Almeida began to prepare the ship for attacking and boarding. He lined the whole superstructure with sheets of copper on the inside so rifle bullets and grapeshot could not pierce it. He obtained two small bronze six-pounders, braced them on the deck with huge boulders picked up on the beach, and placed one on the prow and one at the stern. The weak and timid crew was discharged, and twelve husky, ruthless men were signed on. The regulations were read to them: any disobedience was punishable by death; if they gave a good account of themselves they would be rich in a year and could disembark at any port they wished.

Their first attempt at piracy was against a Swedish craft; she was a bark. They drew close, and the European raised his own flag; the *Relámpago,* a black flag. At once the bark fired six rifle shots which buried themselves in the superstructure, one or two in the foremast. At a distance of thirty feet the *Relámpago* let them have the load of the forward cannon with a terrific blast. Then came the boarding party, and their knives gave no time for the Swedes to reload.

Having seized control of the European craft, they reaped their harvest by looting it. They locked the survivors in the hold and bored holes in the ship so it would sink. The vast expanse of the sea swallowed up their crime.

After three attacks of this kind, Almeida made for Curaçao. When it was dark he put a boat over the side and went straight to the other side of town in search of the beloved source of his suffering. The Igartúas had gone to live in St. Thomas, according to the information he was able to get.

The *Relámpago* set sail for the Windward Islands. It entered the harbor of St. Thomas, and Almeida went ashore to track down the whereabouts of the people he sought. He soon had news of them. Miguel Igartúa had opened up a hardware shop of his own, and had prospered in this business. But he had been in bed for a month with a severe attack of paralysis. The impatient Portuguese went there. Alida Blanca opened the door and exclaimed in anguish:

"Good Heavens! You won't know him when you see him. He's always speaking of you."

"Let's go and see him. . . . Hello, Miguel! How are you getting along?"

"I'm laid up here, useless. And you? What have you been doing with yourself?"

"I've been to sea, my boy, to overcome my grief."

"But José, you're a very handsome fellow! Alida Blanca, see how fine Almeida is looking. Where are you, my dear? I'm going to sea with you, José, to get rid of these blues."

"Whenever you like, Miguel. . . ."

Alida Blanca had heard everything, but she didn't want to go in when her husband called her. And when she heard her husband say he wanted to ship out with the Portuguese, she covered her face and burst into tears.

The doctor came, and firmly opposed the idea of going aboard ship. Igartúa became enraged, and it was necessary to bleed him because he had another cerebral attack. He died during the night.

He had already written out a will before a notary; the document was opened, and it left all his property to his wife.

8

ALMEIDA WENT TO THE CEMETERY to his friend's funeral, and the following day he said to the widow:

"I'm sailing away, and in a month I'll anchor again in the harbor of St. Thomas. Now you are free, and can answer me. Shall I come back or not?"

"Go with God, and return likewise. But first talk with

the priest of my parish in the city, for I'm a good Catholic."

"Good-bye!"

"Good-bye!"

Almeida wanted to respect Alida's grief, and therefore was brief in his remarks to her. Then he went to see the Catholic priest, who told him that one month after the death of a parishioner his widow could not marry again; it was necessary to wait ten months.

"If you don't perform the ceremony," the Portuguese replied, "I'll give up my religion and seek another one." And he told how awkward and difficult his situation was on land, and worse at sea.

"Since it's a special and extraordinary case, I'll perform the ceremony," the priest answered.

9

THE *Relámpago* WAS SAILING close-hauled when she came upon a good prize to windward. It was in the Caribbean Sea, and Alida Blanca was going to witness a boarding attack for the first time. The ship ran up the Norwegian flag and came at the corsair, which raised a black one. She fired a heavy blast at the *Relámpago*, which replied boldly. Then, after the boarding party had lashed the ships together, a hand-to-hand battle with cold steel was fought, and Almeida won as usual. He had twelve men who were twelve wild beasts; five of them had been killed, it was true, but he had massacred all the enemy.

Upon returning to his ship a heartbreaking and appalling sight awaited him: Alida Blanca, between decks, was lying against the foremast apparently asleep or in a swoon. But she was dead, with two bullets in her chest. The exchange of shots caught her there, where she wanted

to witness the bloody battle. . . . She had wanted to see
the fight, but Almeida had ordered her to hide in the hold;
she had answered haughtily, "I am a Basque, and women
in my country aren't afraid of bullets."

The Portuguese shed not a single tear: he unburdened
himself by hurling curses. Then he ordered a course set for
St. Thomas. When he dropped anchor in the harbor he
called Dr. Smith on board. Almeida asked him to embalm
his wife's body with the best chemicals and essences. He
placed her in a glass coffin inside a cedar one, protected by
another made of copper plate.

10

THE PIRATE SET SAIL with his treasure, and buried it on a
small, deserted island off the cost of Puerto Rico. Every
month he would go to visit his dead bride and gaze upon
her lifeless face for hours. . . .

As time went by the crew of the *Relámpago* kept changing gradually, but the pirate captain paid no attention to
this; and every month the faithful Portuguese would go to
adore the countenance of his beloved Alida Blanca. The
personnel of the schooner believed he went ashore to bury
jewels and gold coins. Only the cook and the cabin boy
used to accompany him.

During one of the piratical attacks Almeida made against
Puerto Rico, he was cut off and captured with five of his
crew while curing meat on the shore at Guayama. They
were taken to San Juan, and after a long trial were sen-
tenced to death. The sentence was upheld by the Supreme
Court for Naval Affairs at Havana, for the pirate was
wanted by the British, French and Portuguese govern-

ments also. They were shot by a firing squad at El Morro fortress on February 14, 1832.

I I

WHEN THE BOATSWAIN LEARNED about what had happened in San Juan, he mapped out a plan to recover the treasure of the dreaded pirate. He had taken command of the *Relámpago,* for Captain Trinidad had retired quite some time before that. He sailed south and dropped anchor off the island that Almeida used to visit each month.

They went to the cave where the Portuguese kept the entombed body of his wife. There was a small cross on the ground, and this guided them. They dug down, and one yard deep discovered the metal coffin. The boatswain ordered the digging stopped. He took the lantern and went down to examine the sides of the casket. At this, one of the sailors made a sign to the other, indicating by a gesture that he should hit the boatswain on the head with a crowbar and they would divide the treasure between the two of them.

The scoundrel did so. They threw the corpse to one side, thus saving one third in the division of the spoils. The sailor went down to scratch away the earth around the sides of the casket in order to investigate its dimensions. When it was uncovered and he saw how big it was, the same sailor who killed the boatswain, befuddled by greed, struck his companion on the head and left him lifeless also.

Alone now, the criminal went into the hole to examine the casket slowly, and saw that it had a fine lock with a metal button on it. He pressed the button and the copper cover rose, revealing the glass coffin and releasing a pun-

gent perfume that affected him deeply. The murderer
turned the light upon the coffin, and stood there aghast as
his gaze rested upon a strikingly beautiful woman who
appeared to be asleep. He thought it was witchcraft. The
scent of roses grew stronger. He put his hand to his forehead and found it bathed in cold sweat. Full of mistrust
and gripped by strong superstition, he began to tremble.
The lantern slipped from his hand and went out. He
looked up and saw Captain Almeida, with baleful eyes,
threatening him with a long dagger.

With a mighty effort he jumped from the grave, tripped
over one of the corpses, and staggered. As he put his foot
forward he stepped on the other dead man, and fell senseless to the floor. When he regained consciousness, instead
of walking toward the mouth of the cave he went in the
other direction and fell into a deep crevice, where he
smashed his head.

1 2

THE SAILORS IN THE SMALL BOAT, observing that the boatswain and his two companions did not return, took a lantern and went to the cave in search of their comrades.
When they found the three corpses and a coffin containing
an embalmed woman, they quickly went back on board to
inform the crew about it. The cargo officer went to the
island and brought back to the ship the glass coffin and
the cedar one, in order to give Christian burial in St.
Thomas to the wife of Captain Almeida.

Time went by. A Spanish engineer visited that island to
survey and map it, acting on Government orders. When he
came upon the casket made of copper plate he could not
imagine what it had been used for. The helper who accompanied him told him that it was a traditional belief in

Puerto Rico that the treasure of a Portuguese pirate who had been executed in San Juan was buried there, and that the empty metal chest indicated that someone had dug it up and abandoned the useless copper container. But the discerning engineer, when he drew up the map, decided to call it Coffin Island. And Coffin Island is its name to this day.

Abelardo Díaz Alfaro

1920 -

was born in the town of Caguas, Puerto Rico. After preparation at the University, he taught in the rural schools. (His mother, too, was a schoolteacher, and his father a Protestant minister.) Díaz Alfaro also worked side by side with the jíbaros (Puerto Rican farmers), and came to know their problems very well.

His first literary success was Terrazo (Background of Earth), a series of sketches and pen portraits of life in the rural areas of the island. Published in 1947, it continues to be a best seller in Puerto Rico; the tale we translate here comes from this collection.

The country schoolmaster Peyo Mercé appears in several stories. His attitude toward overemphasis on Americanization of the schools, especially in the rural districts, is viewed sympathetically by Díaz Alfaro and shared by most Puerto Ricans. After all, the island was Spanish for four hundred years, and the Hispanic tradition continues strong today in the Estado Libre Asociado — the Commonwealth —

which has become the cultural crossroads of the Americas.

The teaching of English in the schools has always been a delicate matter. There were many changes before Puerto Rico became a Commonwealth: Spanish for classroom recitations with English-language textbooks used for homework; English compulsory in the classroom, with Spanish used only to clear up points the pupils did not understand (which meant Spanish almost constantly); English used every morning, and Spanish every afternoon; English all day on Mondays, Wednesdays and Fridays, and Spanish on Tuesdays and Thursdays; and variations on these schemes. The obvious result was that the pupils learned neither language really well. Now at last a sensible solution has been reached: Spanish is the official language of instruction, and English is studied as a prescribed subject, like arithmetic or geography.

A nostalgic preference for the Spanish folkways of rural Puerto Rico rather than the new customs of the more Americanized cities — particularly in such matters as the traditional Christmas, when the Three Wise Men bring gifts on January 6th (Twelfth Night) — is as evident in young Mr. Díaz Alfaro as it was in old Dr. Coll y Toste. Puerto Rico remains deeply Hispanic at heart.

"SANTA CLO" COMES TO
LA CUCHILLA

* * *

A PIECE OF RED BUNTING on a bamboo pole marked the location of Peyo Mercé's one-room schoolhouse. A partition down the middle divided the tiny school into two classrooms; over one of them a new teacher — Mister Johnny Rosas — now presided.

Because of a lamentable incident in which Peyo Mercé had made the superintendent appear in an unfavorable light, the latter thought it wise to appoint a second teacher to the district of La Cuchilla so he could instruct Peyo in the newest educational methods and bring the lamp of progress to illuminate that unenlightened district.

He called the young teacher to his office. Johnny Rosas, a recent graduate, had spent a short time in the United States. Solemnly the superintendent said to him:

"Listen, Johnny; I'm going to send you to the district of La Cuchilla so you can take them the most up-to-date techniques you learned in your Education courses. That Peyo doesn't know a thing about it; he's forty years behind the times in the subject. Try to change their ways, and above all you must teach a great deal of English . . . a lot of English."

One day Peyo Mercé saw the fledgling teacher coming up the hill toward the school on an old horse. He even felt a little sorry for him, and said to himself: "Life is probably cutting furrows in him already, just as a plough does in the earth." And he told some farm children to take the harness off the horse and put it out to pasture.

Peyo knew that life was going to be very hard for the young man. Out in the country living conditions are bad, and meals are poor: rice, beans, codfish, and plenty of water. The roads are almost impassable, and always full of puddles. Baths had to be taken in mountain streams, and the only drinking water was rain water. Peyo Mercé had to make his lesson plans by the flickering light of an oil lamp.

One day Johnny Rosas said to Peyo, "This district is very backward; we have to make it over. It is imperative to bring in new things, replace what is traditional. Remember what the superintendent said: 'Down with tradition.' We have to teach a great deal of English, and copy the customs of the Americans."

And Peyo, not very enthusiastic, managed to squeeze out these words:

"True, English is good, and we need it. But good Heavens! We don't even know how to speak Spanish well! And hungry children turn into dull witted little animals. Once the fox said to the snails: 'You have to learn how to walk before you can run.'"

But Johnny didn't understand what Peyo meant.

The tobacco region took on a somewhat livelier mood: the Christmas holidays were approaching. Peyo had already observed with affection that some of his pupils were fashioning rustic guitars out of cedar wood. These fiestas always brought him happy memories of times gone by, and he seemed to hear the Christmas carol that goes

> *The door of this house is open wide:*
> *It shows a gentleman lives inside.*

Johnny Rosas ended Peyo's pleasant reverie with these words:

"This year Santa Claus will make his debut in La Cuchilla. All that business about the gifts of the Three Wise Men on January 6th is growing old-fashioned; it's no longer done to any extent in San Juan. That belongs to the past. I'll invite the superintendent, Mister Rogelio Escalera, to the party; he'll like that a lot."

Peyo scratched his head and said quietly, "I'm just a country fellow who's never left these hills, so the story of the Three Wise Men is right here in my heart. We country folk are sensitive to the things in the atmosphere around us, just as we can smell codfish cooking."

Johnny, by means of class projects, set to work preparing the atmosphere for what he called the "gala première" of Santa Claus in La Cuchilla. He showed his pupils a picture of Santa Claus riding in a sleigh pulled by reindeer. And Peyo, who had stopped for a moment at the threshold of the door between the two classrooms, saw in his mind's eye another picture: an old farmer pulled along on a palm-leaf sledge by goats.

Mister Rosas asked the farm children, "Who is this important person?"

And Benito answered, "Mister, that is the Old Year, painted red."

Johnny was amazed at the ignorance of those children, and at the same time angry at Peyo Mercé's negligence.

Christmas came, and the parents were invited. Peyo held a typical little fiesta in his room. Some farm children sang Puerto Rican songs and Christmas carols to the accompaniment of rustic guitars. And to conclude the performance the Three Wise Men appeared, while an old singer named Simón improvised verses like this:

They come and go from far and near;
We country folk just stay right here.

Peyo handed out traditional rice sweets and candies, and the children exchanged little presents. Then he told his children to file into the room of Mister Johnny Rosas, who had a surprise for them and had even invited the superintendent, Mister Rogelio Escalera.

In the middle of the classroom stood an artificial Christmas tree. Red streamers were stretched from one bookcase to another, and from the walls hung little wreaths with green leaves and red berries. In frosted white letters was a sign that said in English, "Merry Christmas." Artificial snow was sprinkled over the whole display.

The spectators looked in amazement at all this, which they had never seen before. Mister Rogelio Escalera was greatly pleased.

Some of the children went up on an improvised platform and arranged themselves so that they spelled out "Santa Claus." One told about the life of Father Christmas, and a children's chorus sang "Jingle Bells" in English as they shook some tiny bells. The parents looked at one another in astonishment.

Mister Rosas went outside a moment. Superintendent Escalera spoke to the parents and children. He congratulated the district upon such a lovely Christmas party, and upon having such a progressive teacher as Mister Rosas. And then Mister Escalera asked the audience to be very quiet, because soon they were going to meet a strange and mysterious person.

A tiny chorus immediately burst into song:

Santa's coming in his sleigh,
Riding slowly all the way.
Clip, clop! Clip, clop!

Suddenly there appeared at the classroom door the figure of Santa Claus, carrying a pack over his shoulder. His deep voice boomed out in English: "Here is Santa! Merry Christmas to you all!"

A scream of terror shook the classroom. Some farmers threw themselves out the windows; the smallest children began to cry, and clung to their mothers' skirts as they fled in wild disorder. Everyone looked for a way to escape. Mister Rosas ran after them to explain that he was the one who had dressed up so strangely. But this only increased the screaming and made the panic worse. And old woman crossed herself and said:

"Heaven help us! It's the Devil himself talking American!"

The superintendent made useless efforts to calm the people and shouted:

"Don't run away! Don't act like a bunch of Puerto Rican hillbillies! Santas Claus is human, and a good man!"

In the distance the shouts of the fleeing people could be heard. Mister Escalera, observing that Peyo Mercé had been standing there unconcerned, vented all his anger upon him, and shouted at the top of his voice:

"It's your fault, Peyo Mercé, that such stupidity should exist here in the middle of the twentieth century!"

Peyo Mercé answered, without changing his expression:

"Mister Escalera, it is not my fault that Santa Claus is not listed among the Puerto Rican saints."

World Classics in Translation

NEW FRONTIERS OF READING ADVENTURE open up when you explore these expert modern translations of masterpieces of France, Spain, Germany, Spanish America. Language barriers are no longer an obstacle to your full enjoyment of the great literature that you have so long wanted to read. All in attractive editions at modest cost.

from the French

from the Italian

from the German

from the Spanish

6852

Barron's Educational Series
343 *Great Neck Road, Great Neck, New York*